Hounded

June Whyte

A Kat McKinley Greyhound Mystery

Book 3

Books by June Whyte

Sex on Tuesdays

THE GUMSHOE CHICK MYSTERY SERIES

Gone to the Dogs
For the Love of Dogs
Doggone It!

VETS 2U MYSTERY SERIES

Murder at Kangaroo Downs
Death at Dingo Creek
Homicide at Emu Lodge

KAT MCKINLEY GREYHOUND MYSTERIES

Chasing Can Be Murder
Muzzled
Hounded
Leashed

CHIANA RYAN CHILDREN'S MYSTERIES

The Case of the Disappearing Corpse
The Case of the Missing Dinosaur Egg

www.amazon.com/author/junewhytebooks

Hounded

June Whyte

This edition published by White City Press
A division of Misti Media LLC
https://whitecitypress.com
Available in both Paperback and eBook Editions
1 2 3 4 5 6 7 8 9 10
Text Copyright © June Whyte 2024
Cover Copyright 2024 by White City Press
Paperback ISBN: 9781963479423
eBook ISBN: 9781963479270

Without limiting the rights under copyright reserved above, no part of this publication may be reproduced, stored in or introduced into a retrieval system, or transmitted, in any form, or by any means (electronic, mechanical, photocopying, recording, or otherwise), without the prior written permission of both the copyright owners and the above publisher of this book.

The scanning, uploading, and distribution of this book via the Internet or via any other means without the permission of the publisher is illegal and punishable by law. Please purchase only authorized electronic editions, and do not participate in or encourage electronic piracy of copyrighted materials. Your support of the author's rights is appreciated.

To Yolo
(My gorgeous retired greyhound)
Thank you for keeping me company through all the many drafts and re-writes by lying beside me with your legs in the air.

1

C*AN'T STOP THE FEELING…*

My mobile's melodic ringtone yanked me out of a deliciously vivid dream. A dream involving a jumbo-sized jar of gooey chocolate spread, me in nothing but a garter belt, and my sizzling hunk of a boyfriend, Ben, in even less.

I reached across and snatched the persistent mobile from my bedside table. Slammed it up against my ear. "This better be good!" I snarled, as the last image of Ben's chocolate-covered pectorals trickled away. "It's 5 o'clock in the bleeping morning!"

"Katrina?"

Oh God, no! It was my mother…

Okay, most mothers regularly ring their daughters, but my mother wasn't *most* mothers. Firstly, *my* mother, who was busy touring the world with her latest lover, Dwayne the Dweeb—a guy so small and lightweight every time a strong wind blew from the South she had to grab him by the hair so he didn't fly away—had only rung me three times since taking off on a holiday twelve months ago. In fact, I hadn't bothered contacting her when my sister, Liz, went missing, or when we were both in danger from a murderous race scammer. Why? Because Ma wouldn't be all that interested. Anything that didn't relate to Helen McKinley herself, failed to figure high on her list of importance.

"What's up, Ma?" I asked trying to sound upbeat while rubbing the sleep from my eyes and frowning down at Tater, my tea-cup Chihuahua, who was dancing on the floor, the toe of one of my new fluffy slippers in his mouth. "Where are you ringing from today? Hawaii? Greece? A little street-front café in the heart of Paris?"

"I'm ringing from the Sydney airport, Kat. I'm tired. I'm cranky. And I'm waiting to board a plane for Adelaide. The plane is due to arrive at Adelaide airport at 9.00 am, so drop whatever you're doing and be there to pick me up. On time."

"Whaaat?" My heart went into free-fall. I sat up in bed so quickly the room spun. "You're *where*?"

"Katrina Tess McKinley, I do *not* like your tone," snapped my mother adding a loud tut. "Surely it's not too much to ask a daughter to pick her exhausted mother up from the airport after not seeing her for twelve months."

"But-but what happened to Dwayne?"

"Don't mention that name to me. Bastard took off with Betsy Boomer, the Tour Guide floosy and left me in a penthouse in Paris to fend for myself. What else could I do but come home? Well, I can't actually go home as my house is in the middle of renovations, so I'm coming to stay with you for two weeks."

No! No! No! This wasn't happening! It couldn't be. The Universe would never be so unkind.

"And, Katrina," she went on before I could get breath enough to suggest it might be more comfortable for her to book a room in a hotel. "Before you leave to pick me up, throw out any smelly dogs you have inside the house. No way will I tolerate dogs underfoot while I'm staying with you."

I peered down at Tater, one of the 'smelly dogs' referred to, and shook my head at him. Tail wagging, he bounced up and down, dropped my half-eaten slipper on the floor and grinned up at me. Huh. He could laugh. He didn't know who was on the other end of the phone. My stomach did a queasy flip-flop and for a moment I thought I'd have to race to the toilet and puke over the bowl.

And why not?

My mother, Helen McKinley, aka Attila the Hun, was flying into town on her broomstick and intended to stay in my house.

Not for an hour…

Not for a day…

But for two long, challenging weeks!

*****

The sight of my familiar, colorful, *'McKinley Greyhound Kennels'* sign didn't prompt its usual warm, homey vibes when I pulled up at the front of my property. Not today. I clambered out of the car to open the gate. How was I going to survive the next two weeks with my mother added to the already volatile mix? Currently, I had my hippie, anti-everything sister, Liz, and her ex-con boyfriend, Scott, entrenched in my guest room, plus nine of Liz's raucous protester-friends, including two children under five, camped in tents on my front lawn.

Ma could be the live match poised to ignite the ticking bomb.

I could feel my palms growing sweaty on the steering wheel as I drove the car through the open gateway and scanned the driveway ahead. I blew out a sigh. No way could this situation turn out anything but disastrous. After all, when we buried Dad, Ma lost the plot completely, causing Liz, only sixteen at the time, to run away from home and me to move out, put a deposit on my own home, and became a professional greyhound trainer.

Now, for the first time in five years, the three of us would be living together under the same roof.

Yeah. Couldn't wait.

"Well, here we are, Ma. Home sweet home," I said as I parked in front of my fairytale two-story cottage and held my breath waiting for her screams of horror at the sight of unwashed people and the newly formed tent city on the front lawn.

I didn't have long to wait.

"Why are all those dreadful tents on your lawn? And why are those weird people in dirty rags sitting cross legged on the ground smoking pipes?"

"They're friends of Liz."

"Liz?" Her mouth opened. Closed. Opened again. And then set in a grim line. "What is Elizabeth doing here?"

"It's a long story."

At that moment, one of the weird people in dirty rags passed the pipe to the person sitting beside her and slowly got to her feet. Face a mask, she walked toward us. Gave Ma a quick once-over and then glared at me. "What the hell is *she* doing here?"

"Ma, this is your younger daughter, Elizabeth," I said turning to my mother whose eyes were narrow slits. "And Elizabeth, this is your mother." I took a deep breath and two giant steps backward. "Now, I'll leave you two to get reacquainted while I slip down to the kennel house and find Jake. We'll need male muscle power to shift your baggage from the car to the house."

Without waiting to see who drew first blood, I jogged in the direction of the kennel house. Call me a coward. Call me a stirrer. You're probably right. But I'd done my bit by picking Ma up from the airport. Also, I'd be the one giving up my bed. No way could I picture Ma sleeping on the couch. That'd be me. And my back ached at the thought.

I growled deep in my throat and wiped sweat from my eyes as I jogged toward the kennel-house. Boy, it was going to be a very long, uncomfortable two weeks.

"Hi Lofty." I pushed through the kennel-house door and smiled at the big brindle greyhound in the first kennel. Big Mistake, pet name, Lofty, was the largest, ugliest but also the fastest dog in my racing team. He returned my smile, wagged his tail and drooled in anticipation. "Your owner's here," I told him, reaching for the bag of goodies I kept on the top shelf beside my treatment table. Instantly, every greyhound in the dog-shed sprang to life. "But don't hold your breath waiting to meet her," I added as I distributed the treats to every waiting mouth. "'Cos I doubt she'll venture down to see you. God forbid, she might actually breathe the same air as a dog."

When Lofty's previous owner Peter Manning was sent to jail after attempting to fry me in his father's crematorium, I didn't want Lofty to go to another trainer. He was my star performer. So, in begging mode,

I rang my mother. It had taken flattery, untenable promises and a little bullying to persuade Ma to buy Big Mistake. Of course, the fact that she was pissed as a parrot partying in Oslo, Norway, when I rang, helped my cause. But even drunk, Ma retained the upper hand. She bought the dog on one condition—if he didn't win back her outlay, plus a fifty percent profit in the next twelve months of racing, I'd reimburse her the full purchase cost.

Ma never saw the dog. Had no intention of watching him race. And this didn't worry me in the slightest. Big, ugly, Lofty, the greyhound with the personality of a best-friend and the heart of a dragon, still headed my racing team.

"Jake! Jake! Where are you?" I left the temporary kennel house and went hunting for my dreadlocked assistant. A guy in his early twenties, Jake was only one step up from the protesters smoking weed on my front lawn, but he was a good worker and brilliant around the dogs. They all loved him and I could leave him in charge without a qualm when I went off racing, because Jake cared for the greyhounds as though they were his own.

"I'm over here, dude."

Dressed in baggy yellow trousers and a purple tank top, Jake was directing the workers who'd arrived that morning to build my new brick kennel house. A flash of white teeth and several silver facial studs greeted me as I joined him. He cocked his head to one side and listened. "Like, is that a fight starting up near your house?"

"Umm…possibly." I nodded, closed my eyes and tried to filter out the angry voices and occasional high-pitched screams. "My mother's arrived home from a world-tour and decided to stay with me for two weeks." I heaved a long drawn out sigh and rubbed a hand over my eyes. "The whole situation's a disaster, Jake. Unless *you* can help me."

His eyes grew large and he tugged at one dreadlock, his fingers twitchy. "Hey, man, I'm not, like, doing any refereeing. No way. I'd be a dead man. I'm no good to your dogs, like, without all my body parts."

"Jake, I just want you to keep an eye on them for me. That's all. I have to go to the races with three dogs in half an hour."

Jake's face paled. "Keep an eye on them? Without being squashed like a bug?" He puffed out a breath. "How?"

I shrugged. "Look, just ring me if things get out of hand. That's all."

Jake frowned. "Keep watch, like, from a distance?"

I nodded.

His grin returned. "Hey, that's okay, dude. I can do that. Like, as long as you don't want me to put my nose anywhere in the house, I'm your man."

"Thanks, Jake. You're the best. Now, if you could just help me carry Ma's luggage from the car to my bedroom…"

"But, man, you just said, like—"

"Pretty please? I wouldn't ask, but she's got a thousand cases and my back hasn't recovered from lugging them into the car at the airport."

With a huge sigh of resignation Jake followed me up the path to the front of the house.

One hand on the handle of the car, I looked around. Frowned. Normal activity in Tent City, but no sign of Ma or Liz out the front. Hmm…maybe they'd killed each other and the protesters had buried them under the front lawn.

Holy catfish! What was I thinking? I closed my eyes and sucked in a deep breath while counting to ten. Yep! I was definitely losing it.

Before Jake and I could start unpacking the car, Liz came storming through the front door with her friend, Tinkerbelle, one of the older, more strident and vocal protesters of the group. Both were waving their arms wildly. I'd experienced more than a little trouble with Tinkerbelle since she'd erected a tent on my lawn—the largest, of course—and immediately declared herself Queen Bee of Tent City.

I narrowed my eyes at her. What was the woman cooking up with my sister now?

Liz and Tinkerbelle flounced across the lawn, and when they disappeared inside Tinkerbelle's tent, Jake rolled his eyes to heaven and opened the back door of my station wagon. "Trouble brewing there," he declared and reached for the first two cases.

"Hurry up, Katrina! Take my luggage up to my room…and be careful." Puffed out like a bantam rooster, Ma exploded through the front door and strode toward us. "And what did I tell you about those smelly dogs? I've shooed them out the back door and I don't want them anywhere near me while I'm visiting."

Biting back a strong desire to 'shoo *her* out the back door', I let out a growl of pent-up frustration, and reached inside the car. Bloody woman. Maybe I would unfold a camp stretcher in the kennel house and stay there until she left.

Before I could drag the first case from the car, the loud-mouthed Tinkerbelle, who looked more like the Wicked Witch of the North than Peter Pan's ethereal fairy friend, pushed open the flap of her tent and strode across the lawn toward us.

I froze. This could turn ugly.

Stringy thin build, straw-like hair down to her backside, expression like she'd sucked too long on a bottle of vinegar, the woman came to a halt in front of us. "Hey, you!" she said and squared up to my mother. "I want to talk to you."

Of course, Boadicea-On-Speed puffed herself out and squared right back at the woman wearing green rubber boots and a long flowing skirt that dragged in the mud. "And *you* are?"

"Tinkerbelle. I'm the Earth Mother of this camp."

Ma, eyes travelling imperiously up and down the woman in front of her, sniffed and lifted her nose in the air. "Judging by the dirt on your clothes, I can see how you got *that* title."

Tinkerbelle snarled. "At least I'm not a pathetic, rubbish mother." She leant forward, inches from Ma's face. "And I don't send poisonous toxins into our midst, like you."

Ma gasped. "Poisonous toxins?"

"Yeah, worse than poisonous toxins. You're radiating an inverse complexity that transcends the Universe and seeps into the World of Darkness below."

Ma made circling motions beside her head with one finger. "And you, you're crazier than a headless chicken doing the can-can."

"Now, come along, ladies…" I began, in what I hoped was a placating voice. "Let's not say things we don't mean. If we're going to make life pleasant for everyone, we need to stop squabbling and live in peace." I took hold of Ma's arm and tried to drag her toward the front door. "Um…how about a nice cup of tea?"

She shook me off as though I was an annoying insect and fronted up to Tinkerbelle again. It wouldn't have surprised me to see her put up her dukes and get into a boxing pose. "Hey, Earth Mother, if I stunk of rotten garbage, like you, I *would* expel poisonous toxins." Ma's high-decibel screech sent two nearby white cockatoos, careening off towards the hills.

"And if I had a stick up my ass so far it poked out my nose, like you, I'd stop breathing and make life a lot more pleasant for everyone else in the Universe. In fact, someone should stake you out in a pit of poisonous snakes. The world would be better off."

Oooh! Now she'd done it!

Ma's chest pumped out to its full size, 40 DD, and she stepped right up into Tinkerbelle's space. "Yeah, and someone should bash you over the head and switch off your lights. Permanently." She pushed forward into the other woman with her ample chest, rocking Tinkerbelle backwards. "And…if that's a large sign on your back saying, 'please dispose of me'…I'd be happy to oblige."

By now, the other protesters, including Liz and Scott, were gathered on my front lawn, seemingly to cheer on the two combatants. And, except for the two littlies hiding behind their mother's long skirt, the others were treating the verbal altercation as entertainment.

Jake and I exchanged sideways glances as we each grabbed two cases from the car and scuttled toward the house. Okay, I'd tried to break up the fight. No-one could accuse me of not attempting to prevent the War of the Dominatrix. But it was a lost cause. So, as things looked like turning even uglier, and I was allergic to blood, I left my long haired, metal-enhanced assistant to carry in the rest of Ma's luggage.

While I took off for the safety of the Gawler race-track.

2

GAWLER GREYHOUND TRACK, SET IN THE heart of the now ultra-busy town of Gawler and edged by a river that resembled a dry creek-bed, seemed peaceful after the anarchy at home. Nothing to celebrate in the races so far, though. *Pedro's Popsicle,* the maiden dog I'd boxed in the first race had finished seventh out of a field of eight. Starting from box five, the squeeze box, he'd been wiped out by the rest of the field the moment he jumped.

At a window-table in the newly-finished upstairs cafeteria/conference room/viewing area, my best friend, Tanya Ashford, and I sat hunched over a large plate of chips, liberally doused with tomato sauce and vinegar. Of course, I'd filled Tanya in on the latest disaster relating to my surprise visitor, plus said visitor's altercation with the camp's Earth-mother-cum-harridan, Tinkerbelle.

"So," Tanya lifted her voice as the babble around us grew louder, "they were both still fighting when you left?"

"Like Ali and Frazier."

"What? The Thrilla in Manila—and you walked away?"

"What else could I do with three dogs racing here today." I shrugged. "Even if I'd stayed home to referee, neither Ma nor Tinkerbelle would listen to me. I'm just an annoying mosquito they'd like to smack, instead of the person who owns the house they're guests in."

"Well, I've already told you what to do. Be. More. Forceful." Tanya dipped a chip in the sauce and transferred it to her mouth. "You're far too obliging, Kat. People always take advantage of nice people." She picked up another chip and waved it at me like another finger. "It's time you told those blood-sucking parasites to pack their tents and go hug trees somewhere else."

"Yeah. Yeah. I know." Tanya was right. It was time to dump my nice-girl persona and drag Bombshell Chick out of retirement. "I'll have a word with my darling sister when I get home." I chewed on a chip and tipped my head at my friend. "Anyway, what are *you* doing at the track today? How come you're not at the shop selling battery-operated panties to some bearded guy with tattoos?"

Tanya worked at the Adult shop in the little town of Virginia where she sold everything from high-powered vibrators to human-sized blow up dolls.

"Flexi-day. Knew you'd need a bit of company with Lover-boy in Melbourne racing his dogs, so I popped over for a while."

I raised my eyebrows at her. "Since when did Norm believe in flexi days?"

"Don't worry, it was given grudgingly." Tanya gave a sharp laugh. "What happened was, my esteemed boss got himself accosted by an angry customer last week and the poor guy needed the rest of the day off to get over the trauma. I ran the shop on my own while he was recovering. Hence, he *had* to give me today off."

"An angry customer? Can't see *Norm the Nervous* developing the balls to make anyone angry." Norm was the most unlikely person to run an Adult shop. He was shy, easily embarrassed and a devout Catholic. The sort of person you'd be more likely to find running a Bible shop than *The Luv Bug*.

"Yeah. Poor Norm. Although it was funny—in retrospect. See, this big hairy biker guy stomped into the shop demanding a replacement for a blow-up Barbie he'd bought the day before. And when Norm told him that tying the doll to the back of his Harley and driving through a ring of flames didn't constitute normal wear and tear, the guy went ape-shit."

"*Uh! Oh!*"

"Yeah. *Uh! Oh!* By this time, Yours Truly was hiding under the counter in the Dildo Department wetting her pants and getting ready to dial 000." She rolled her eyes. "Long story, short, when the tattooed biker decided to show Norm his lucky knuckle duster, complete with blood stains he hadn't got around to cleaning off, and even shoved it in Norm's face so he could get a closer look, Norm decided *the customer is always right* was a policy worth following." Tanya wiped tomato sauce from her lips and tossed the tissue on the empty plate. "Let's just say, the biker-guy walked out of the shop five minutes later on the arm of a brand new Barbie."

I almost choked on a saucy chip. Just then, my cell rang. "Damn. Bet it's Jake again." I dragged the phone from my back pocket and checked caller ID. Yep. This was the third time my dreadlocked dude-helper had rung since I left the house an hour-and-a-half ago. With a shake of my head, I stuck the phone to my ear. "What's up, Jake?"

"Dude, your Ma and that witch-woman—they're at it again."

"And?" When I'd conned Jake into keeping me up-to-date with any likely problems among my dysfunctional guests, I hadn't meant a minute-by-minute report.

"They're like, in the kitchen, dude, and your Ma's threatened to hurl a pot of hot stew over the freaked-out witch if she doesn't fly away on her broomstick."

I sighed. My life had gone down the toilet and I'd need more than the fire brigade to rescue me. "Well, did Tinkerbelle leave?"

"Dude, she's, like, put this cool curse on your ma."

"What do you mean, cool curse? Did she turn Ma into a tarantula?" I could see Tanya's eyebrows hitching upwards along with the corners of her mouth. Okay for her. She didn't have to walk through my front door later today and sort out this mess.

Jake blew a sigh through the phone. "No, man, but she, like, cursed your ma's hair. Said it would drop out, man, and she'd be like, totally bald."

I couldn't help it. I laughed out loud. "Oh, Jake, curses aren't real. And even if they were, at least she didn't turn Ma into a little green man with webbed feet. Look, go back to the kennel house and make yourself a cup of herbal tea. Put your feet up for half an hour and relax. You deserve it. I'll talk to Liz tonight and see if she can get them all to leave. Okay?"

I clicked off the phone and turned to glare at the still-grinning, Tanya. "Hey, you can laugh. The Wicked Witch of the North and Queen Boadicea-On-Speed aren't living with you."

"But, a curse?"

"Yeah, been a few of those flying around the house since Tinkerbelle arrived. She tried to turn me into a slimy toad with giant warts the other day. Didn't work, of course, but I swear I had a craving for fresh fat flies for the next 24 hours."

I glanced at my watch. Time to rug up *Enjoy a Schooner* and stretch her muscles ready for the next race. Leaving Tanya to finish off the rest of the chips, I scraped my chair back and stood up. *Enjoy a Schooner*, or Suzy, as we called her at home, was a white and black greyhound with the bubbly personality of a blonde. A ten-man syndicate from the local pub owned her, so if she won today, I'd wager there'd be a few sore heads in the morning.

Come on Suzy!

Fifteen minutes later, collar and lead dangling from one hand, I stood behind the metal starting boxes with the other seven handlers. And as the lure powered up and whizzed past, I held my breath. Heard the metallic ping of the lids as they flew open.

Come on Suzy!

I could see the little white and black greyhound up lying second. So far so good. As the dogs rounded the first turn, I grabbed another breath...and let it out on a disappointed whoosh. Looked like the day was set to continue the way it started...down the plughole. Sandwiched by outside runners drifting in and inside dogs spearing outwards, Suzy was shunted back through the field to last. Poor girl didn't stand a chance.

Oh well, at least we'd take home a large bag of *Hounded*, the new super-duper greyhound formulation, which had recently come on the market. The manufacturers were donating a bag of their product to every dog that came in last at Gawler today. Their message was: 'Last today—but with *Hounded* on the menu—your greyhound could be first past the post tomorrow.'

Oh yeah. And horses might fly…

I tugged the little white and black dog off the lure, did the collar up around her neck, and told her what a good girl she was. Main thing—Suzy was still full of smiles and looked like she could have gone around again.

"Congratulations," I told the trainer of the winner as we walked side by side back to the kennel house. "Top run by your dog today. Won in good time too." I didn't add that with an 8, 8, 7, 8 beside the dog's form, it was no wonder he'd started at the long odds of 50/1.

One more race and we could go home. Not that I was actually looking forward to that prospect. Home at the moment was where crazed, angry women had taken up residence.

As I left the kennel-house I felt an insistent vibrating buzz emanating from my back pocket. Not again. I dragged out my phone and clicked on the incoming text-message.

Going back to my pad. Tinks and your Ma throwing stuff at me. Jake x

I rammed the phone back into my pocket. Time to put a lid on my problems at home and focus on my next race. Wonder Boy, or Clark, as he was known to his friends, should get a trouble-free run in the eighth race and turn the tide back in my favor.

Two of Clark's owners, Marjory and Bob Sanders, both residents of the RSL Aged Care Facility that syndicated Clark, were waiting for me. A lovely old couple, the husband and wife team always showed up to watch their dog race, while the other residents at the Home watched him run on Sky television. They all knew the dog personally because once a month I drove Clark to the Aged-Care facility for a Pat-a-thon. Or that's what the residents called it. Clark visited every person in the Home and laid his head on their lap while waiting for his pat and small treat. The elderly men and women enjoyed it, Clark's tail never stopped wagging, and it made my heart sing to see the love in the eyes of the residents as the dog approached.

"Kat, darling, how are you?" Marjory greeted me, arms outstretched. "You need to eat more," she added, as usual, enveloping me in a bear hug that smelt of talcum powder and vanilla perfume. "I keep telling you, too much work and not enough play results in one skinny girl. Next time I'll bring you a box of our wonderful cook's scrumptious cream cakes. That'll put some meat on your skinny bones."

Marjory's hugs were always full-on and bestowed with love. How I wished Ma would take hugging lessons from this gorgeous woman. "Not sure I need more meat on these bones, Marjory, but I won't say no to the cream cakes." Still grinning, I turned to her niftily dressed husband, Bob. At 82, Bob was so spritely and fit you wouldn't guess he'd suffered a triple bi-pass only two years before. "Hi, Bob," I said. "Did you watch Suzy's race?"

"Yeah, we made it just in time." Bob leaned in and planted a kiss on both cheeks. I could smell strong peppermints on his breath. Bob never went anywhere without a bag of peppermints tucked in a pocket of whichever coat he happened to be wearing. "I thought she had a good chance when she jumped so well, but then, like the poor old swagman who jumped in the billabong, her luck changed for the worse. Oh well, guess you can't win 'em all."

"Can't win 'em all?" I repeated, grinning as I sent him a cheeky wink. "As long as your boy Clark wins, hey?"

A toothless smile lit up Bob's craggy eighty-two-year-old face. "He's special that dog," he purred. "And today I have a pocket full of two-dollar coins from the other residents to bet on him. On the nose."

"And what a job that was—collecting two dollars from everyone," put in Marjory, raising her eyebrows as she shook her head. "They're a bunch of tightwads, that lot. Love collecting the dividends when Clark wins but haven't the strength to undo the zippers on their purses when it comes to laying out the money."

Bob rattled the coins. "Tell you what, girls, I'll be relieved to get rid of these. The weight in my pocket is giving me an old-man's limp."

"And we can't have that, can we?" Marjory cut me a wink and then hooked her arm through her husband's. "See you at the winning post, Kat."

I gave them a thumbs-up and smiled as they strolled off, arm in arm, in the direction of the course TAB. Their dog, Wonder Boy, was a striking fawn youngster who would have gone close to winning this year's South Australian Derby if my kennels hadn't been burnt down by a mad-man, a week before the race. Today, in a much easier field, he was a short-priced favorite to win. I blew out a sigh. The way my day was going, even the results of Clark's race would be in the lap of the Gods. And the Gods certainly weren't favoring me so far. Instead, they were led by Thor, the dark threatening Thunder God, and Kronos, who ate all his children except Zeus, who, when he grew up, chained Prometheus to a rock and ordered an eagle to peck at his liver every day for eternity.

Not the sort of Gods you'd bring home for dinner…

An hour later, I followed the kennel steward along the narrow aisle to row eight and waited for her to undo the security lock on Clark's kennel. Geez, he was keen to get going today. If I hadn't been prepared for the 38kg punch in the chest, the dog would have slipped past me and gone off to get himself ready for the race.

"Clark!" I admonished him as he dragged me to the rug rack, where I selected an XL white rug. He'd drawn box 3 in his race. "If you don't behave, I'll put you back in your kennel and then you won't get to race with the other nice dogs."

He wagged his tail and continued to bounce up and down with a grin on his face. Evidently didn't believe a word I said.

Legs one each side of his body, I slipped the white rug over Clark's head, then maneuvered first the right front leg then the left into separate leg holes. Not easy when the dog between your legs is bucking like a rodeo champ.

Before I could finish, he decided it was time to pee. So, not waiting for me to pull his rug down across his back, he dragged me from the inside of the kennel house to the outside. And if he'd been human, I reckon he would have moaned in pleasure as he cocked his leg and watered the nearest fence post.

"Did you hear about the mystery illness?"

I spun around. It was Trina Sullivan, one of Ben's ex lady-friends. Usually she acted like I was enemy number one because I'd had the audacity to steal Ben away from her, but today, concern etched her thickly made-up face.

"Mystery illness? What do you mean?"

"Greyhounds are getting sick and no-one knows what's causing it," Trina said, walking her greyhound beside mine. "Dogs are okay one day—then they've got a sky-high temperature the next." She shook her head. "Doug Frazer's dog, he died."

At that moment, the lure went roaring past for the preview and I needed to focus all my attention on Clark, who kept leaping shoulder-high in the air. He wanted to run. A big strong dog, it took all my strength and concentration to prevent him from slipping his lead and chasing the lure before the race even started.

With Clark on an ultra-short lead, I followed the red-rugged one dog, and the checkered number two dog toward the 531 meter boxes, my mind on what Trina had disclosed. Greyhounds getting sick? Doug Frazer's dog dead? Geez, I'd need to find out more about this mystery sickness before I left to go home.

In single file, we led the dogs up the race-track another hundred meters and then turned and headed back to the boxes, ready for the start.

"Two, four, six and eight behind the boxes," yelled the starting-steward. Of course, being an odd number, Clark resented waiting his turn. He was all for pushing his way to the front of the queue. I held him back on an even shorter lead.

"One, three, five and seven behind the boxes."

As I stood behind box three, collar and lead off, one arm under Clark's stomach and the other around his neck, ready to lift him into the box, my mobile began vibrating in my back pocket. Buzzing like a hive full of bees. We weren't allowed to use our mobiles while handling the dogs, so I'd turned my phone onto vibrate before entering the kennel house.

"One, three, five and seven in the boxes, please."

Ignoring another urgent vibration that had my phone almost leaping from my pocket, I boxed Clark, slid the back door down and moved away to make room for the handlers in the back line to come forward and box their dogs.

The green light blinked on. The lure powered past. The lids pinged open.

But where was Clark?

I groaned out loud. Couldn't believe my eyes. Clark, usually an excellent beginner, had gone up with the lids and missed the start by six lengths.

Damn!

At that moment, the phone juddered insistently from my pocket again. I banged the heel of my hand against my forehead and swore. Not only were the mythical Greek Gods, Thor, Kronos and Zeus against me, but so was the entire Universe.

Dragging my feet toward the catching pen, I slipped my phone from my pocket and surreptitiously jammed it against my ear.

"Dude, you'd better come home…"

"Jake, I *can't*…."

"But man, your Ma's been into the cannabis cookies."

"Can't *you* keep an eye on her?"

"But she's taking off all her clothes…"

"Oh…"

"And now, she's, like, chasing the postman and the guy delivering pamphlets up the road and…"

"You're right, Jake. I'd better come home."

3

Half hour later, I tumbled out of my car and peered at the colorful sign on the wire mesh gate at the front of my property. Something was different. There, after the printed words *McKinley Greyhound Kennels*, some smart-ass had painted a crude cartoon picture of two dogs copulating. And the female dog had a face like my mother.

No time to admire the art-work however, as from somewhere near the house, I could hear what sounded like either Indian war-whoops— or the last call of a dying wolf. With a sigh that came from deep down near my shiny black shoes, I climbed back into the car and drove up the driveway to find the cause of the noise, Tanya tailing me in her little red Yaris.

It was not a pretty sight.

There in the middle of my front lawn, around a desultory camp fire made up of half a dozen smoldering sticks, an alien creature danced. I gulped. Blinked. And all that covered the alien creature's saggy, womanly bits was a thin layer of streaky wet mud.

"She's totally blitzed!" Tanya, already out of her car, choked on a muffled giggle. "Your mother's higher than the 7.30 Qantas flight on its way to Brisbane."

"That's *so* not funny," I said and wriggled out of my coat. "Here, help me get this on Ma before someone sees her."

"Bit late for that." Tanya's giggle turned into a snort. "She's already chased the postman and the guy who delivers pamphlets off the property and I reckon they got quite an eyeful in the process."

"Very funny. Not." Feeling every one of my twenty-eight years, I strode toward my cavorting mother, coat held out in front of me in an attempt to partially hide the view. "Come on, Tan, give me a hand to put my coat on her."

"Um…I'm sort of a bit freaked out about touching all that wet wrinkly skin."

"Alright for you. It's *my* mother's wet wrinkly skin we have to touch!"

As Ma danced past, I grabbed her arm and tried to stuff it in a coat-sleeve. "Quick, Tan! Grab the other arm!"

"Can't! She won't let me!" Tanya yelled back. "Almost got me in the nose with her fist that time."

Ma, too wet and slippery for me to secure a firm grip, pulled away and continued to dance. I sighed, sucked in another deep breath in preparation for a second attempt. Then, as she pranced past, doing a fair imitation of a middle-aged Hiawatha, I grabbed her by the arm and held on. "Easy Ma," I said in what I considered a soothing voice. The voice you use on a psychotic dog that's barked itself into a delirium. "It's okay now. I'm home. I'll look after you."

She jerked away from me, fear and revulsion in her eyes. "Get away from me! Don't touch me!" Spittle flew from her open mouth.

I shook my head and narrowed my eyes at her. Why did I even bother?

"Hey, Mrs. Mack, remember me? Tanya Ashford. I'm a friend of Kat's. I used to come and sleep over at your place when my parents went away on business."

I threw Tanya a grateful look. She caught it and sent back this 'you owe me big-time' grin.

Ma approached Tanya as though she were a long-lost friend. "Hello, Tanya, dear. Aren't you looking beautiful today? Your face. It's glowing. What shade of purple is that?" She patted Tanya's face then looked down. "Oh, but your shoes, dear. They're pretty shoes, but way too big. I can't believe how big your shoes are." Her eyes widened and she leaped backwards, one hand covering her mouth, both boobs bouncing. "They're still growing! Quick! Quick! Take your shoes off! Take them off, or they'll swallow us whole!"

"Ma, you're hallucinating."

Ma shook her head, a deep frown creasing the skin between her eyes, her hands dancing up and down like agitated fire-flies. "No, no. Look at Tanya's shoes! If we don't hide, they'll eat us!" She grabbed my hand in a vice-like mad-woman's grip and dragged me toward the nearest tent. Feet digging in, I struggled to get away, but it was like bracing your weight against a cement pole. "Come on, child, we have to hide before the shoes find us." And then, without warning, she let go of my hand as though she'd been holding a burning hot coal.

Of course, without the forward pull to balance my backward resistance you can guess what happened next.

Yep. Fell on my bum, right in the middle of Ma's sorry-excuse-for-a-fire. Luckily, by this time, the pitiable fire had given up the ghost and it was mostly smoke and ash.

I grit my teeth in a parody of a rictus grin and took a deep breath. Shrugged. Only a couple of weeks and I'd have my house back. Only fourteen days. 336 hours. 20,160 minutes. I gulped. Hey, I could cope with that.

From ground level, I watched Ma bend over and pick up a blade of grass from between her feet. She examined it in meticulous detail, her frown disappearing. Her eyes softened, then lit up with joy as she gently stroked the blade of grass. She smelled it. Stroked it. Reveled in its structure. Geez, you'd have thought she was holding the Crown Jewels in the palm of her hand instead of a blade of grass. "Exquisite," she purred. "Beautiful. Gold and silver and sparkly like fireworks at Christmas." She smiled and shook her head. "Perfection."

"Jesus!" Arms folded, Tanya shook her head at me. "What are we going to do? Your Ma's away with the fairies."

"Find Jake." I heaved myself off the ground and brushed myself down. "Jake smokes marijuana all the time. He'll know what to do." Leaving Ma, buck naked and waxing lyrical over her blade of grass, Tanya and I dashed along the path toward the kennels. "Jaaake!!" I yelled. "Where are you?"

"Over here," he answered from the foundations of my new kennel house. "I'll be with you as soon as I've like, shown this dude where to dump his load of sand. The workmen have finished for the day. Boss sent them off-site."

"Okay. But we need your help with Ma. Urgently."

"Oh, man, I don't have to, like, touch her do I?"

"I'll wrap her in a blanket."

Jake didn't look convinced, but once he'd finished directing the site-manager, who dumped a load of sand before taking off again, he followed us along the path back to the lawn and stood watching Ma as she sat cross-legged in front of the fire.

"Like, where's the blanket?" Jake pulled a face, and then covered his eyes with both hands.

"Okay, okay!" While Ma sat quietly stroking and having an in-depth conversation with her blade of grass, I snaffled a dog blanket from the car and wrapped it around her body.

"You can look now."

Jake opened his eyes and shook his head at Ma. "Reckon she's been getting stuck into the cookies—not smoking."

"But where did they come from and who fed them to her?"

Jake, mind still on the effects of marijuana cookies, screwed up his nose. "I remember the first time I got stoned," he said, his voice far away. "There was this gnarly tree in our backyard that seemed to like, come alive. Scared the crap outta me." He scratched at one of the metal rings in his left earlobe, eyes thoughtful.

"But will Ma be okay, Jake?"

"Yeah, dude. She'll be fine. Just needs to sleep it off."

So, with Jake on one side, me on the other and Tanya opening doors and hitching the blanket up whenever it slipped, we half-dragged, half-lifted Ma up the stairs and into my bed. She lay there, quilt pulled up to her chin, gazing at the ceiling as if it bore the complete works of Leonardo da Vinci.

I shook my head at the goopy look on Ma's face and turned to Jake. "Where's that witch, Tinkerbelle?"

"Dunno. Must be around here somewhere." With an uneasy shrug, he cast his eyes around the room. Probably worried Tinkerbelle might burst out of the wardrobe and turn us all into rolls of toilet paper. "But, you know, like, I haven't actually seen her for a while."

"Maybe now Tinkerbelle's accomplished her mission, she's gone into hiding." I looked down at the confusion on my mother's face and frowned. "And the way I'm feeling at the moment, she'd better stay hidden."

Ma moaned and covered her ears with both hands. "Go away," she groaned. "You're disturbing the *little people*."

I rolled my eyes. "Little people?"

Jake grinned. "You know, like fairies and gnomes and Lilliputians and maybe a Hobbit or two."

"Smart-ass!" I fake-punched Jake on the arm and then glanced down at Ma who was now relaxing against the pillows, a faraway smile on her face. "Well, we can't do much more here, so we'd better get back to work. While you get the three greyhounds out of the trailer and let them lose in the emptying yards, I'll make up the dog-teas."

"No probs, dude."

"And I'd better push off too," Tanya added as she followed me down the stairs. "But, hey, if you need me, or just want someone to vent to, give me a call. I'll be home all night."

"Thanks, Tan. Looks like Ma's going to sleep it off now, but if I find out who did this, we'll hold a party."

"What sort of party?"

"A Payback Party. We'll scarf a few Coronas first, and then, while you hold the perpetrator down, I'll put on a funny hat, blow a noisy party-whistle and then get to work with the tar and feathers."

4

I WAS ELBOW DEEP IN WARM, SOAPY WATER, washing the thoroughly-licked dog bowls, when I heard the protesters' rusty Kombi van back-fire, clatter through the front gateway and continue to shake and rattle up the driveway. The van wasn't nicknamed The Rattler for nothing.

"Jake," I called out. "Can you check the dogs have their night-time rugs on before you go home? My sister's back and I want to tear a few strips off her before she and that lazy boyfriend of hers dive head-first into their bedroom and lock the door." I shook my head as I grabbed a towel and wiped my hands. "Even rabbits don't go at it as much as those two."

"Sure, dude." Jake grinned at me. "Unlike you and that muscle-bound boyfriend of yours?"

I grinned back at him. "Okay, okay, I admit it. I miss Ben, crazy bad." I screwed my nose at him. "Shows, does it?"

Jake nodded. "Sure does, dude. But don't let the lack of going at-it, like, hijack your sense of humor."

"What do you mean?"

"To be honest, dude, you've been like a bear with a toothache since he left."

"I have?"

"Yeah, man. Mary Poppins got it right, you know," went on the young dreadlocked sage. "Laughter *does* make the medicine go down."

He lifted his eyebrows and smirked. "Even if the medicine *is* spiked with marijuana."

I threw my head back, took a deep breath, and closed my eyes. Jake was right. Of course. Somewhere in the midst of housing an activist sister with a penchant for noisy lovemaking but not housework, a lawn covered in crazy activists, the thought of Queen- Boadicea-on-Speed here on a two-week, unwanted visit, and the love-of-my-life, dark-eyed, six-packed, Benjamin Taylor in a hotel room, over a hundred miles away from me…

Yep. I'd colored my world in black and it was affecting my mood.

I looked around at the contented faces of my dogs, all fed, rugged and settled for the night and a sense of contentment wedged itself in my chest. I really had a good life. Lofty banged his tail on his bed to get my attention and then smiled at me. One ear up, the other drooping, Roman nose, feet splayed like a claw bath. Not the face a photographer would likely display on a greeting card, but Lofty the greyhound was blessed with the temperament of a favorite friend. I gazed outside at my long runs and galloping paddocks and at my picture-post-card house at the end of the track. I surveyed the cleared ground where my new kennel house would eventually be built.

I had it all.

Taking a second look at the cleared ground, I couldn't see any workmen. Weren't they supposed to finish cementing the floor today?

"Hey, Jake, what did you say happened to the work-men?"

"They started mixing cement for the kennel-house floor after you left to go to the track but the Boss-man sent them off-site."

"Why?"

"Reckoned he unearthed a piece of asbestos in the rubble of the old kennel-house and told the men to go home while he investigated."

"Asbestos?" I shook my head. "There was no asbestos in the old kennel house."

"I tried to tell him that, man. He said it was to do with Health and Safety regulations and then after dropping off that load of sand, he took off too."

"Hope they decide to get back to work soon. Be great to have a brick kennel house again." I stacked the last of the dog bowls on the table and headed for the house. "See you in the morning, Jake. And thanks for sharing your Mary Poppins quote with me."

"Cool, man."

"My grumpy mood has been duly noted, but won't change until *after* I've spoken to Liz. I wouldn't be surprised if she was in on the Get-Ma-High stunt with her sneaky friend, Tinkerbelle."

Surprisingly, Liz was waiting for me when I strode into the living room. I thought I'd have to knock down the bedroom door, close my eyes to what was going on inside and drag her downstairs by her hair. Instead, she was slouched on the settee, legs crossed, Tater, my spunky Chihuahua on her lap and Lucky stretched out on the floor at her feet. She looked up expectantly when I came through the doorway and grinned up at me. "So…you couldn't put up with Ma's bellyaching any longer? Hey…didn't think you had it in you."

I narrowed my eyes at her. "What are you talking about?"

"Didn't you show Ma where the cannabis cookie-jar was hidden before you left for the track today?"

"Liz, I don't know where you and your sidekicks hide the cannabis cookie-jar. In fact, I didn't know there *was* a cannabis cookie jar. If I did, I'd have dumped the contents in the garbage bin." I let out a sigh and softened my voice. "Liz, I know you and Ma don't get along, but–"

"Don't get along?" she broke in, color rising in her cheeks. "Jesus, Kat, half the time Ma doesn't even acknowledge that I'm her daughter. When I heard her singing in your bedroom, I went in and found her kneeling on the bed singing to the ceiling. And you know what she said when she looked up and saw me there? 'Elizabeth, you're looking more like your mother every day.' What the hell did she mean by *that*?"

I shrugged. "Liz, we're talking about a woman who is high as a kite. Someone whose best friend is a blade of grass. And just to be sure here—*did* you slip her something illegal before you left to champion the termite population?"

Liz shook her head. "Nah. Probably would have, if I'd thought of it, but hey, our mother was her normal overbearing self when I drove off with the others. She and Tinkerbelle were still threatening to turn each other into slimy, giant centipedes as we rattled down the driveway."

"Didn't you think it strange that Tinkerbelle didn't go to the rally?"

"Not really. Tink's more into climate change and the warming of the planet than tearing down termites' homes." Liz lifted one shoulder and grinned. "Maybe after we left *she* offered Ma the cannabis cookie-jar, you know, as a peace-offering, making sure, of course, they were the double-strength variety we put aside for 'special' occasions."

"And now she's conveniently holed up somewhere safe, afraid to come out and own up to drugging our mother."

"Tinkerbelle is afraid of nothing, Kat. When the Gods created our Earth-Mother, they smashed the mold."

"Huh. Smashed it because they realized they'd created a monster."

"You take that back, Katrina. Tinks, she cares about us."

"Okay, well, where is she now? I haven't laid eyes on the woman since I got home."

Liz frowned. "Did you look in her tent?"

"Ma and I actually *hid* in Tinkerbelle's tent when Tanya's shoes were chasing us, evidently with the intention of eating us."

Liz rolled her eyes heavenward. "I'm not even going to ask you to elaborate on that weird statement."

"And this was *before* Ma began having an in-depth conversation with a blade of grass, and *after* she thought she was Hiawatha's spirit, performing a war-dance around a smoldering camp-fire."

My little sister suddenly looked as tired as I felt. She blinked up at me with a *'this isn't what I came here for'* expression on her face. I sympathized with her. Hey, taking care of a ranting, spaced-out mother is out there with preventing a recalcitrant toddler from playing dodgem cars on the main highway.

I'd run out of steam too. I flopped onto the settee beside Liz. Of course, this prompted Tater to immediately change laps and Lucky to jump up beside me and snuggle her nose under my left arm-pit.

I let out a long, drawn-out sigh. "What are we going to do, Liz?"

"Think it might be time for me and my friends to move on. There's a big rally coming up in Townsville, Queensland, at the start of next week. Everyone worth knowing will be there. All to do with the horrific methods the Queenslanders use to murder cane toads."

I blinked at her. I was actually talking about Ma, not Liz and her gang, but this latest cause warranted further explanation. "Um…and how do you *want* the Queenslanders to murder the cane toads?"

"More humanely. Of course."

"But they'd still be dead, so does it really matter?"

"Of course it does!" Liz jumped to her feet and waved her hands in the air. "You have no idea the good we do with our causes, do you? If it wasn't for us, snobby horse-people would still be riding to hounds and killing foxes."

"Okay, I get your point. Your passion for noble causes is to be applauded." I took a breath, prepared myself for the fallout before continuing. "However, foxes are now in plague proportions. They're killing baby lambs and chasing the chickens in the farmer's hen-house."

Liz scowled and stamped her foot. Reminded me of Tanya's eleven-year-old daughter, Erin, whenever Tanya confiscated her mobile phone. "Don't worry, big sister," Liz growled. "We'll all be out of your hair first thing tomorrow morning. Then you and Ma can play happy families together without her crazy, no-account younger daughter bringing down the value of the neighborhood."

"Liz!" I called out as she stormed up the stairs, probably to wind down by having a noisy bout of sex with Scott. "I'm not asking you to leave. You can stay here as long as you like. You're my little sister, and I love you."

"Not your fault, Kat. I love you too, but I refuse to stay anywhere within a hundred miles of *that woman*. My friends and I'll be gone in the morning."

"But Liz…"

She threw me a cheeky grin when she reached the top of the stairs. Then, slowly, brazenly, tugged her sweater off over her head and stepped out of her jeans. "Don't worry, sis," she said, dropping the discarded clothing on the landing floor and opening the bedroom door. "We'll all be back in time for Christmas dinner."

5

An hour later, after feeding Tater and Lucky and the two GAP dogs that lived by the front gate, then feeding myself with a frozen dinner loaded down with calories and preservatives, I returned to the kennel-house.

Unfortunately, racing dogs did not treat their own injuries. Trainers were in charge of that.

With my mobile phone tucked between my shoulder and my right ear, I sat hunched on a green hard-plastic kindergarten stool, beside the treatment table, one arm under Lofty's chest, the other hand fastened to his left leg which was immersed in a bucket of ice water. I'd tied the dog's lead to a table leg, praying if he decided the water was too cold and made a dive out the door for freedom, the table wouldn't disappear with him.

"What are you wearing?" It was Ben's voice on the other end of the phone. *My* Ben. The Ben I'd tried everything—including handstands on the hood of his car—to catch his attention earlier in the year, and still couldn't believe we were an item—in a monogamous relationship—full-on boyfriend and girlfriend, in every position of the Kama Sutra. And now, even though he was miles away racing his dogs in Melbourne, I could tell, with those breathless words, 'what are you wearing', his mind was locked in on sex. With me.

I glanced down at my clothes, worn for working in the mud and cold, and grinned. "Baggy jeans, a red and white flannel shirt and a roll-neck sweater," I told him, holding back a laugh. "Oh yeah, and my grungy rubber boots. You know, the ones that always rub a hole in the bottom of my socks."

Ben's sigh echoed down the line.

"Hey," I said. "I'm dressed for treating dogs—not for hopping into bed."

"Couldn't you just fib a bit? Give me a bit of a thrill and make stuff up? I don't want to hear about grungy rubber boots that rub a hole in your sock. I want to hear about you naked."

I swallowed.

"Here I am, sitting here in my hotel room, all by myself, thinking of you and believe me, babe, in my mind, you are *not* wearing rubber boots. As for your jeans and shirt and sweater—I've ripped them off and tossed them out the window."

I laughed, dropped the phone, startled Lofty, who pulled his foot out of the ice-water and stood staring at me with a defiant, but gooby look, that clearly said: *If you think, for one moment, that I'm going to put my foot back in that bloody ice cold water—you're dumber than you look!* I scratched him behind the ears and moved the bucket to safety. Guess I'd finished icing his tendons for tonight.

"You've caught me at a bad time," I told Ben once I'd rescued my phone. "I'm in the middle of treating dogs. I've just finished icing Lofty's tendons—he pulled up a bit sore last start—and still have to ice Clark's shoulder and treat Suzy's track-leg. Can I ring you back later?" I put on my sexiest voice…well, I reckon it's sexy, but Ben says I sound like I've got a frog in my throat. "Later, when I'm undressing, very slowly, and getting ready for bed?"

"Ooh…" Ben's voice broke up. Yep! This time I'd got through to him. I grinned. It felt so powerful knowing I had this hold on the gorgeous Benjamin Taylor. Although, to be honest, I was getting a bit damp in the nether regions myself, just thinking about slowly undressing, one piece of clothing after another, exclusively for him.

"And maybe," he went on, his voice a gravelly whisper, "*before* you pull on those hideous flannel pajamas with the baby ducks all over them, send me a selfie—you know, just to keep me warm tonight."

Oh boy!

"Only if you send me one of you getting out of the shower."

"Katrina. You're doing my head in," he growled. "How many days before I come home?"

"Hopefully you'll win the final of the Ballarat Cup in a week's time and arrive home, pockets bulging with money. And," I said, letting my voice go a bit croaky, "I thought we could play doctors and nurses to celebrate."

His swallow sounded louder than a Bernard Tomic serve. "Jesus, Kat, I don't know if I *want* to qualify for the final. Don't think I can last another week just on phone sex, when all I want to do is run my hands over the real you, lick every crevice and…oh, God, I gotta go. Ring me later, when you're going to bed."

I hung up, a goopy smile on my face. Benjamin Taylor loved me— or at least he loved my body—and couldn't wait to get back into my bed. Still thinking of Ben, bed, and Kama Sutra sex, I put Lofty away with a treat and snapped the lead onto Clark's collar.

The only way I'd last another week without Ben was by busying myself with day-to-day activities at home.

Which brought me back to the depressing fact that I had a domineering mother flat on her back in my bed, high as a kite, a group of unwashed hippies camped on my front lawn, and now, according to my sister, Liz, two of her protestor friends had disappeared. Tinkerbelle couldn't be found. And Babette, a man-eating, lusty woman of indeterminable age, who always appeared to be poking her large boobs into the face of both available and unavailable men, had disappeared while participating in their latest protest march. Liz was worried. Me? My views on the subject were, hey, they're two fully-grown, consenting adults and if they decide to take off for whatever reason—that's their business.

All greyhound-treatments completed for the day, I passed around a bag of liver treats, one for each open mouth, closed the kennel-house door, locked it, and pulled the collar of my sweater up higher around my neck. Breathing in the cool air, I heard the deafening sound of rhythmic banging down in front of the house. Must be Mary. Every night she banged this damn gong-thing with an iron bar to bring the others together around the camp fire for their evening meal. I stood a moment longer in front of the kennel-house, gazing around my property, taking in the softness of early evening as it settled over the trees and paddocks, and smiled.

Hey, while I was lucky enough to live here, doing what I loved, I could cope with anything. Very soon, Ma and Liz and the protesters would be gone. And in a week's time Ben would be home.

Still smiling, I whistled my two pets, Lucky and Tater and my current GAP dogs, Yolo and Ralph who'd joined the other two on their nightly fossick.

Two black greyhounds raced toward me, tails wagging so hard their bodies swayed from side to side. Yolo ran straight past while Lucky came to a bouncing stop in front of me. Barked. Then turned around and went racing off again. She repeated this two more times. "What's up, Luck? Where's your other two mates?" I frowned. 'Where's Tater?" Something was worrying Lucky and I couldn't see hide nor hair of either Ralph, the white and black GAP greyhound, nor my little brown Chihuahua with the heart of a Stegosaurus. The little brown Chihuahua who was probably nose deep in some sort of mischief at this very moment and goody-four-shoes, Lucky, had decided to dob him in.

Eyes bright, Lucky cocked her head to one side, listening to every word I said, and then promptly galloped off again, peering back at me every few strides to see if I was following. She headed in the direction of the old burnt-out kennel-house that was now surrounded by bricks, piles of sand, and a marked-out base ready for the workmen to hopefully start pouring cement in the morning. My heart missed a beat and I started to run. Maybe Tater was in trouble. Maybe he'd fallen down a hole the workmen had forgotten to fill in. Or maybe some of the loose bricks had fallen off the top of the pile and buried him.

"Tater!" I called, as I drew nearer to the building site. "Stop messing around. Come on out. It's time for your doggy biscuit."

Expecting him to hurl himself at me, eyes shining, mouth open in a yes-please-let's-go-eat grin, I slowed down and searched the site, my eyes alert for any movement.

"Tater?"

He was digging at the base of the load of sand that had been delivered after the workmen had finished for the day. Ralph was running in circles around him. Barking frenetically. What were they up to?

"Tater, stop that!" I yelled. "You'll end up in China if you keep digging."

As I drew closer to the building site I could see Tater had made a hole in the side of the sand, his little feet digging faster than a beaver, his nose completely buried in the sand and his tail a ticking clock on high-speed, while Lucky, satisfied that she'd done her job, ran from side to side beside Ralph, barking, but not joining in. Yolo, enjoying her freedom, had disappeared somewhere up the back of the property. She'd come when she heard the rattle of the biscuit tin.

By now, it was almost six o'clock and the light was fading fast. Time to get these guys settled for the night and watch some mindless television. I stepped past Lucky who was still bouncing up and down like a yoyo and moved toward Tater. If he wouldn't come voluntarily, I'd have to pick him up and carry him into the house.

"Come on Tater. Biscuit time." Tater's excited yapping grew more frantic. What on earth had he discovered? A buried ball? A bone? One of my old shoes? Or maybe even a rat?

"Tater! Leave it!"

The little dog glanced over his shoulder at me and then stepped back, a smug self-satisfied grin on his pixie face, as though presenting me with the Crown Jewels. Intrigued, I peered down at the hole he'd dug in the sand. At the *thing* he'd been worrying with his sharp little teeth.

The *thing* protruding from the sand pile.

And couldn't drag my eyes away from it.

I tried to huff a shallow breath, but the breath caught in my throat, almost choked me.

This wasn't happening. It couldn't be. Not again…

Panting for air, my mouth shot open in a gurgling scream that didn't go anywhere. My stomach heaved, then hurled regurgitated chips and gravy all over my rubber boots. My legs, suddenly wonky, didn't want to hold me up, but no way was I going to let them dump me beside the sand pile.

I squeezed my eyes closed. Counted to five in my head. Blinked them open.

And looked down…

There, spilling from the yellow sand, was a bloodied hand. A hand with multiple rings on the fingers. And the hand was attached to an arm with the words PEACE tattooed on the inside. And around the wrist were a series of colorful bracelets made out of sea shells.

Looked like I'd found Tinkerbelle.

6

A LITTLE OVER AN HOUR LATER, Detective Inspector Garry Adams of the Elizabeth Police Precinct strolled from my kitchen into my lounge room, his long, daggy overcoat flapping against his legs as he walked. Short, scruffy, a twin to Colombo, the laid-back detective from that 80's television series of the same name, Adams looked as if he hadn't been home to shower and change since the last time I'd had a run-in with him. Six weeks ago.

"Is that the last one, PC Stevens?" he asked the constable standing sentry by the kitchen door as Mary, the final suspect to give a statement, dropped onto the settee beside her two sleeping children, her face wet with tears.

"Yes sir. And except for Mrs. Helen McKinley, they all claim to have water-tight alibis."

I exchanged a quick glance with Liz and bit my bottom lip. I could see things were going to get nasty. And had no idea how to save the situation.

DI Adams, leaning against the lounge-room wall, rummaged in his coat pockets, pulled out a worse-for-wear cigarette, reverently sniffed one end and then carefully returned the treasure to its original lodgings. For later? To stall for time? To remind him of lost pleasures?

Then, ever the dramatist, he narrowed his eyes, and from under bearded eyebrows, surveyed the faces of every person in the room. Ma, bowl of popcorn on her lap and head drooping on her chest as she tried to stay awake, Liz, her mouth set in a grim line as she and Scott squeezed into one of the lounge chairs together, Mary, still crying, Mystique and Spirit, better known as the *Woo! Woo! Twins*, due to their airy-fairy view of the psychic phenomena, and the other two protesters, Sienna O'Lachlan and Greta Schultz. Babette, the woman who hadn't returned with them from the march, still hadn't been located. Finally, DI Adams' eyes came to rest on me. I sat on the floor, legs stretched out, back against the wall, with Tater on my lap and Lucky curled in a ball beside me.

Under the detective's relentless gaze, I tried hard not to squirm, but couldn't help the instinctive nail-biting, as I stared back up at him.

"Tell me, Ms. McKinley," he began, his voice mock-conversational, his head with its mop of uncombed, overdue-for-cutting, dark hair tipped to one side. "How is it that so many dead bodies seem to find their way into your vicinity?"

I took my fingers out of my mouth and carefully studied my bitten nails. Wished the floor would open up and swallow me.

"Thing is," he continued in that smart-ass voice I'd come to expect from him. "It doesn't seem to matter where you are—inside the house—inside someone else's house—and now, inexplicably, outside your house. If there's a body within sniffing distance, you'll uncover it. Why is that so, Ms. McKinley?"

What the detective forgot to add was that every time I found a body he tried to pin the blame on me. And it was getting old.

I shrugged one shoulder. "I have absolutely no idea," I told him. "It's not like I go looking for them."

He tilted his head to the other side, bushy eyebrows raised. "Yet, they can hardly come looking for you."

Smart-ass.

He wasn't finished. Not by a long shot. "So, tell me, Ms. McKinley, why were you near the building site at that time? And why, specifically, beside the load of sand?"

I let out a sigh of resignation. I'd already been through this line of questioning, three times and counting. "As I've already told you, and a couple of your henchmen, Detective, I'd just finished treating my racing dogs, locked the kennel-house door ready to come inside the house and discovered one of my pet dogs was missing. This one." With a shift of my chin, I indicated Tater who looked up, gave his fans a cocky, I'm-a-superstar grin, and bowed his head as though waiting for applause. "I found Tater digging in a pile of sand one of the workmen had delivered this afternoon. And when I looked closer, I-um-I discovered Tinkerbelle." Prickles ran up my spine and my breath hitched. I shifted on the hard floor and continued. "Well, Tinkerbelle's hand. Well, actually, the whole arm. It was sort of poking out of the sand." Throat clogging at the awful memory, I started scratching behind Tater's ear for comfort. "Straight away I knew it was her because of the tattoo and her distinctive shell bracelet. Anyway, after a short time, when I could move again, I-I felt for a pulse…" The thought of that cold dead flesh under my fingers had my stomach churning. Again. Not that there could possibly be any chips, gravy, or boxed chicken and vegetables left to eject. I took several shallow breaths before continuing. "But there *was* no pulse. So, I rang you."

DI Adams swung around to face Ma, who had fallen asleep, the bowl of popcorn upside down on her lap. "Was Tinkerbelle, real name Mrs. Patricia Brown, the woman, *you*, Mrs. McKinley threatened to kill earlier in the day."

Ma woke up, slowly raised her head and blinked at the detective, confused. Ever since we'd dragged her out of bed, dressed her, and brought her down the stairs to the lounge room, all she'd been interested in was eating and sleeping. A side-effect of over-consumption of marijuana, so Liz informed me. "Um…pardon?"

DI Adams blew air out through his mouth, then bent to carefully brush at the creases in his trousers. Creases that were merely a long-forgotten memory. "Earlier today, Mrs. McKinley," he said, every word enunciated loudly, clearly and slowly, as though Ma was either five years old or ready for a nursing-home, "you were heard to threaten the deceased. In fact, I have six witnesses who will swear on the fur of an endangered species, that you and the victim, Tinkerbelle, as you know her, had a full-blown argument. An argument in which you threatened to…" He gave his note book an exaggerated shuffle before squinting down at the top page. "Now, what were your exact words again? Oh yes. Here it is. 'If that's a large sign on your back saying, 'please dispose of me'…I'd be happy to oblige'." And another quote. 'Someone should bash you over the head and switch off your lights, permanently.'" He drew himself up to his full height and sent Ma a grim-lipped smile. "Which, incidentally, is exactly the modus operandi used in this murder."

One of our mobile phones, confiscated the moment the police had arrived and bundled together on the coffee table in the lounge-room, vibrated loudly until it finally ran out of puff, took a breath, and then began vibrating again.

The DI puckered his forehead. "Well, don't just stare at it," he snapped at the policeman nearest the table. "Check the phone out. It could be useful to our investigation."

I closed my eyes and cursed the Gods, the Universe and all things related to technology. The madly vibrating phone was mine. Of course. And I'd bet my next month's house-mortgage payment on who and what was on the other end of the line.

The constable picked up the phone, studied the screen and I could see his teeth biting into his bottom lip. Probably to stop from rolling around the floor laughing.

"Well, come on, Constable, what's up?" DI Adams reached one hand out and grabbed the phone from him. "Anything to do with the case?"

"Um…no. I don't think that's likely, sir."

DI Adams eyeballed the image on the phone, raised one eyebrow in either surprise or admiration and his gaze sliced across the room to rest on me. "Hmmm… you're right, Constable. Nothing to do with the case but…um, *something* is definitely up." He turned the phone off and laid it carefully back on the table with the others.

I closed my eyes and imagined icy winds, snow, and vanilla ice-cream. Didn't work. Judging by the deep burn beneath my skin, my face was now fire-engine red. No way could I ever let Ben discover his latest selfie could well-be a topic of discussion at the local cop-shop for years to come.

I watched the muscles in the detective's face twitch and contort until he had himself under control again. Then, after one last sideways smirk at me, he began pacing up and down the room. Finally, he stopped and swung around to face Mary, who'd been covering her two sleeping children with a blanket. "Ms. Larson, where exactly were you when Ms. McKinley's mother threatened the victim?"

Mary looked up, wiped her nose with the sleeve of her sweater then glared at Ma. "I was standing no more than three feet away from the two of them." She sniffed, used her sleeve as a handkerchief again. "And then *that* woman," she pointed at Ma, "*that* woman threatened to kill my best friend in the whole world."

"Only after your *best friend in the whole world* threatened to kill my mother." I yelled at Mary, scowling at the woman who for the last month had been happy enough to pitch a tent on my lawn, use my facilities and my kitchen to cook hot meals for her children. "They were *both* arguing. *Both* threatening to kill each other."

"But only one of them is dead," DI Adams pointed out.

"Okay, but it was just talk. Bluster. And anyway, Tinkerbelle wasn't Mary's best friend. Tinkerbelle used to drive Mary mad with all her wacky ideas on how to bring up kids."

Ma, unperturbed by the accusations and reproachful glares hurled at her like sharp stones at a stray dog, eyed the upside-down bowl in her lap, then thoughtfully transferred a handful of popcorn from her lap to her mouth and began to chew, slowly, while studying the life-line on her right palm. Apparently she had no intentions of defending herself. Or maybe she couldn't remember what day it was, let alone whether she'd whacked Tinkerbelle with a shovel or not.

"What are you implying, Detective?" I said, getting to my feet and spilling a disgruntled Tater onto the floor. "If you're accusing my mother of murder, you must be out of you mind. If my mother hit Tinkerbelle over the head and killed her, how could she get the body from the house to the building site? Are you saying she suddenly developed the muscles of an Olympic weight-lifter and carried, or dragged the body all that way, then shoveled a load of sand over her?"

"No. The killer used a wheelbarrow to transport Mrs. Brown's body up the path to the building site."

"How do you know that?"

"We found traces of blood inside a wheelbarrow left on the building-site. And it's only a matter of time before forensics confirm that the blood belonged to the victim."

My chest tightened. "Oh." I dragged in another breath before glancing across at my mother who had eaten all the popcorn and was now using a mouth-wet finger to spear the last of the crumbs. *Could* she be a murderer? Had she been so high on drugs at the time she didn't know what she was doing? "Um…well…it's still the same argument. How did she get the body *into* the wheelbarrow?" I persisted, glowering at Liz who hadn't opened her mouth once to defend Ma. "My mother isn't what you'd call, fit and strong. It would be impossible for her to lift Tinkerbell's body into a wheelbarrow."

"Nothing is impossible when you're dealing with a resourceful killer, Ms. McKinley. In fact, most murderers can be quite creative when they put their mind to it. A little old lady who looked as though one puff of wind would blow her away was convicted of murder just last week. She'd killed her husband, a giant of a man, and stored his body in the freezer."

My expression must have shown my disbelief as he continued with his grizzly tale. "So…how did this small woman lift her husband's body into the freezer, you ask?"

No. Not me. I'm not asking. I'm *definitely* not asking…

"By using an axe that hung in the garden shed and chopping her husband into chunks. Chunks light enough for her to lift, bag, and stack."

Oh my God. The detective's tale had sent a hundred little

hobgoblins, all armed with sharpened pitchforks jouncing around inside my stomach. They were playing chasey. Or paint-ball. Or maybe even a re-enactment of the War of the Roses. Which was exactly why I *didn't* want to know the answer to the detective's bloody Grimm's fairytale in the first place. I gave my stomach a soothing rub and drew in a deep breath. "Okay, you've made your point, Detective, but in this case, the victim wasn't cut into chunks. Tinkerbelle was still whole."

DI Adams produced a set of workman-like handcuffs from his back pocket and swung them from side to side, as though impatient to fasten them on someone's wrists. "I'm just describing how murderers think, Ms. McKinley." His dark eyes, chips of coal, took on a menacing gleam. "Murderers don't think like normal people. In fact, some killers I've put away would have made top CEO's if they'd applied their brilliance to the general workplace, instead of criminality. Some are so clever they'd have already found the cure for cancer if they weren't so busy running around shooting people or working their way up to the top of a drug empire, by eliminating the opposition."

Adams shuffled across the room and came to a stop in front of Ma, towering over her like an eagle over its prey. She blinked up at him, eyelids heavy as though she'd love nothing better than to curl up in bed and sleep for a week. As though she was only waiting for this crass, rude man to leave the house so she could disappear into the bedroom with another bowl of popcorn and maybe a hamburger-with-the-lot, eat until she felt sick, and then crash-out on the bed.

But DI Adams wasn't ready to leave. Not yet. And not without a trophy. He shuffled a step closer, open handcuffs still swinging. He cleared his throat before speaking. "Helen Jane McKinley, I am arresting you on suspicion of the murder of Patricia Brown. You have the right to remain silent but whatever you do say can and will be taken down as evidence and used against you in a court of law."

7

I don't know which was worse. Watching Ma being handcuffed and led to a police car or seeing Tinkerbelle entombed in a black body bag, strapped to a gurney, and wheeled toward a silent ambulance.
With Lucky pushing up against my leg on one side and Tater voicing his opinion in staccato yaps on my other side, I stood at the front door, unable to stop the movie-like action from enfolding on my gravel driveway. I shivered. A deadly cold had crept into my bones and invaded my mind.

After Detective Inspector Adams had read Ma her rights, Constable Stevens led her to a police car, politely placed a hand on her head and helped her climb into the back seat. During this embarrassing ritual, my mother had no idea what was going on. Her eyes were blank, her smile was fixed and she probably thought the nice constable was taking her for a ride in the country to commune with more blades of grass.

However, Ma would be steaming-mad when the effects of the drugs wore off and she woke up in a jail cell the following morning. She'd flip—big time. I shivered again, tugged my coat closer around me. I guess it was up to me to do some sleuthing. Ask the hard questions. Find out if Tinkerbelle had any enemies with a good enough reason to bash her over the head and hide her body in a pile of sand.

Of course, my sister, Liz, refused to help. All Liz cared about was her next cause. In this case, the toxic cane toads of Toowoomba who were being beaten to death with cricket bats and golf clubs, instead of the more humane disposal of bagging and freezing. Though if I had the option of being hit for a six with a cricket bat, or a slow death via freezing, I'd opt for the quick splat every time.

Anyway, when DI Adams insisted Liz and her anti-everything pals stay put until the investigation was completed, they found themselves in a no-win situation. If they stayed, they'd miss the cane-toad rally in Toowoomba. If they defied the detective and left, they'd be arrested for not cooperating with the police. Liz and Scott, complaining of police brutality, locked themselves in my guest-room, while the rest of the antis disappeared into their tents to contemplate their next move.

Which is why I stood outside my best friend, Tanya's house at 10pm, half an hour after the authorities had transported both Tinkerbelle and Ma to their separate accommodation for the night.

"Let me in Tan! Ma's been arrested for murder and I need your help." I banged my fist on the door, then when she didn't answer within ten seconds, jammed my finger on the door bell and left it there. I could hear the dying screams of a rat caught in a trap echoing through the house. Tanya's idea of a jokey door-bell chime.

The door opened and Tanya, wearing flannel pajamas with little Martians cavorting over them and cute fluffy bunny slippers, blinked a welcome. "Murder? Your mother?" She shook her head, bewildered. "The last time I saw your mother she was lying on your bed talking to the ceiling. And according to her, the ceiling was answering back."

Tanya's huge hairy lurcher, Petunia, came skidding down the passageway, her rope-like tail wagging an exuberant welcome. I grabbed at the door frame and held on. From six feet away, the big gray dog lurched herself at me, woofing in delight. This was Petunia's usual way of welcoming friends to the house, which is why most of Tan's friends suggested catching-up at a local coffee shop. If I hadn't secured my grip on the door frame, I'd have ended up flat on my butt on the floor.

"Petunia's pleased to see you," observed Tanya, rewarding her monster-of-a-dog with an ear rub, instead of a strong telling-off. She closed the door behind us and led the way into a well-lived-in open-plan kitchen/lounge area. "Well," she said heading for a large refrigerator covered in magnets and unholy drawings of vampires and werewolves, presumably created by Tanya's eleven-year-old daughter, Erin. "If I'm going to help break your Ma out of jail, guess I'll need a bit of Dutch courage, first." Tanya opened the fridge door, bent down and grabbed a six-pack from the bottom shelf. "Why don't you go park yourself in your favorite chair?" She grinned over her shoulder at me. "That's if you can move Sweetie without shedding blood."

"Firstly, I don't care if your evil cat has first claim on my chair—he's off. And secondly, we are NOT going to break Ma out of jail."

"We're not?"

"No, of course not. We just need to find the real killer so the police can release Ma from jail. Legally."

"Oh, is *that* all?" Tanya, six-pack in hand, pony-tail swinging, rolled her eyes. "Silly me, I thought we were planning to do something, you know, *dangerous.*"

Ignoring Tanya's jibe, I made my way across the thick multi-colored carpet to the warmth of a flickering open fire and dropped into Tanya's big old faded green armchair. My favorite chair. It wasn't just cozy, it had the added bonus of smelling of cats, horses, dogs and my best friend, Tanya. It was my own personal security blanket.

Naturally I had to dump Sweetie, Tanya's huge ginger feline that looked more tiger than house-cat, off the chair first. Fortunately, the now-spitting cat was asleep at the time so I managed to empty the chair without losing any skin. From the floor nearby, Sweetie narrowed his eyes at me and growled. Okay, he was cranky. So…what was new? I snuggled into the chair and leant forward warming my hands by the fire. There was always a clash of wills between me and Tanya's grumpy cat, whenever I wanted to sit in my favorite chair.

"Okay, I'm ready." Tanya plunked the six- pack, plus two glasses on a coffee-table between the two arm-chairs. "So, what's this about a murder?" She looked across at me and must have seen the answer to her next question. Her face went white. "Oh no…don't tell me *you* found the body?"

I nodded and ignoring the glasses, yanked a bottle from the six-pack, unscrewed the top, attached the lip to my mouth and upended the bottle. Oh yessss! As the amber liquid cooled my throat and trickled into my stomach, I closed my eyes. It didn't matter how long I lived, I would never ever get used to eyeballing a dead body. Okay, this one wasn't as bad as the other two I'd discovered because most of Tinkerbelle was buried in the sand when I found her, but it was still a dead person. Someone who'd had her life snuffed out as easily as blowing on a lighted match. I took another even larger swig of beer. Who would do such a thing? What evil could snatch away the one thing we all treasured over everything else in the world?

Tanya sank into the other big old chair by the fire and leant across to relieve the six-pack of another beer. She twisted off the top. "And who was your mother supposed to have murdered? That fascinating blade of grass she was strangling when I left?"

"Tinkerbelle."

"Whaaat? The Wicked Witch of the North?"

I nodded. Took another gulp of cold numbing liquid. Let the alcohol do its job. "Problem is, Liz's hippie-friends told DI Adams about the heated argument Ma had with Tinkerbelle earlier today. Told him Ma threatened to bash Tinkerbelle over the head and kill her."

"Was that how she was murdered?"

I nodded again. Let out a breathy sigh of frustration. "If I owned a crystal ball, I'd never have left the two of them together. I'd have scratched the dogs from the Gawler meeting and stayed home. But how was I to know things would escalate? That Ma would somehow get high on drugs and Tinkerbelle would get herself killed?" I placed the half-empty bottle back on the coffee table and turned to Tanya. "Meanwhile, there's a murderer running around out there—the real killer—and we have to find out who he or she is. Ma may be many things, a lousy hugger, a bully and a pompous snob, but she'd *never* commit murder."

As I leant forward to push Petunia's inquisitive nose away before she connected with my crutch, my mobile rang. I tugged it from my back pocket and studied caller ID. Immediately, a comforting warmth filled my chest, making me smile. It was Ben.

"Hi sexy," I purred into the phone, ignoring Tanya's eye-rolling smirk. "Loved your wet and wild selfie. Especially Trigger. That boy looked cocked and ready to go for a long exhausting ride."

"He's in the stable now but I could always get him out for you. Take a video. Maybe show you how I get the boy all saddled up, ready for a gallop."

I squirmed and crossed my legs. "Not now, Ben. Please. I'm not alone—I'm at Tanya's house."

"Tanya's?" His voice lost its sexiness. "What the heck are you doing there? I've been going crazy waiting for a selfie of you getting ready for bed. What's going on?"

Tanya leant across and yelled into the phone. "She's found another dead body, Ben. Your girlfriend just can't help herself."

"Please…tell me she's joking."

"Wish I could."

"Who's dead?"

"Tinkerbelle. The loud-mouthed anti. Tater found her under a pile of sand and tried to dig her out. I rang 000 but when the police arrived they arrested Ma because the hippies ganged up and told DI Adams that Ma threatened to bash Tinkerbelle's head in."

"Bloody hell!" Ben's voice went up an octave. "Look, I'll come home straight away. If I leave Melbourne now, I'll be home by morning."

God, I loved this guy. Any other boyfriend would be ranting and raving and threatening to lock me in my room next time he went away. Not Ben. He'd willingly give up the chance of winning big prizemoney interstate with his dogs and travel home to be with me when I needed him. "No, Ben. I appreciate the thought, but there's nothing you can do by being here. Just stay where you are and win some races. Okay?" I'd give anything to see Ben's gorgeous face but he needed money to extend his kennels and I had to stop being a big girl's blouse and stand on my own two feet. "By the way, how did your dogs go in the heats of the Ballarat Cup tonight?" I asked him. "I was sorta busy at the time being badgered and harassed by the charming DI Adams and couldn't watch or listen to your races."

"Two dogs in the final next Wednesday, but I can leave them with my mate, Paul, and come home. Paul can train them for the final."

"Benjamin Taylor, you stay right where you are. I'm not made of porcelain. I'm more of a chunky-metal type. I can look after myself."

He laughed. "Chunky metal? Now that's not exactly the image that comes to mind when I think of you. More along the lines of soft, smooth, sexy…"

"Enough! You're doing my head in…"

"Only your *head*? Hey, I can do better than that," he interrupted, his voice suggesting more than I could cope with in front of Tanya.

"Ben, I'm going to put you on speaker now so Tanya will hear every word you say. Okay? We're in the middle of planning an attack."

"So, it's step aside Xena—here comes Chunky-Metal—Warrior Woman."

"You can cut out the sex-talk you two, and listen to me." Tanya tapped the base of her empty beer bottle on the table, her voice thoughtful. "I've been thinking…"

"Always dangerous," put in Ben.

"If your Ma threatened to bash Tinkerbelle's head in, and that's what actually happened," continued Tanya, ignoring Ben. "Whoever murdered Tinkerbelle must have heard the argument." She paused for effect. "Otherwise, how would he or she know exactly how to implicate your Ma?"

"Good point," I said. "Which means he or she must have been within hearing distance when they were arguing."

"Or passed the information on to the killer." Tanya, who'd already swallowed the contents of two bottles, picked up another. "What about

Tinkerbelle's hippie friends? Could one of them have done her in?"

I shook my head. "Nah. They all have alibis."

"Convenient," put in Ben.

"Iron-clad though, I'm afraid."

Tanya frowned. "Don't tell me your little team of antis were sitting arm-in-arm across a roadway, preventing buses from bruising the bitumen, and a grumpy policeman came along and took their names?"

I grinned. "Close. They were sitting, arms linked together, encircling a termite-infested tree, somewhere in the city parklands. And yes, a grumpy policeman *did* take their names when they refused to move."

Tanya snorted derisively, upended her third bottle of beer, and let the fiery liquid gurgle down her throat.

"Plus, when questioned by DI Adams, after I'd discovered Tinkerbelle's body, they all insisted Tinkerbelle was their Earth Mother and could do no wrong." I shook my head. "But I don't go along with that either. I've been watching the group while they've been camped on my lawn and seen and heard the supposed, Earth Mother, throwing her weight around. She was definitely the boss-cocky and not everyone took her bullying without protest." I screwed up my nose, thinking. "Take Mary. She's the wishy-washy hippie, the one with the two little kids, Jamie and Charlotte."

"Yeah, I know the one you mean," said Ben. "She's the ding-a-ling that sits cross-legged in the middle of your driveway, staring at bugger-all for an hour. Calls it meditating. Meditating? Christ, she didn't even move when I drove through your gate and headed straight for her. Be interesting to see what would happen if she accidently sat on a bull-ant's nest. Wonder if she'd continue meditating then?"

"Ben, don't be mean," I said into the phone. "Anyway, Tinkerbelle had this bad habit of interfering with Mary's kids. Personally, I think Mary does try to be a good mum. Must be hard on your own. But when The Big Bad Witch interfered, with her weird ideas of what parenting *should* be about, she had the two little ones bawling their eyes out in no time." I frowned. "Doesn't make sense. Mary and Tinkerbelle were constantly at loggerheads, yet when the DI questioned us, Mary acted as though Tinkerbelle was half-way to sainthood and the world had ceased to function now she was with us no more."

"Hmm…" mused Tanya, "do you think maybe Mary got sick of Saint Tinkerbelle's interference and staved her head in?"

"Can't be her. Mary was at her mother's house all afternoon. She couldn't have been in two places at once."

Ben's voice came through the phone again. "Could this Mary character have employed a hit man?"

"Unlikely." I laughed. The gentle meditating Mary doing business with a gun-toting hit man didn't compute. And then I thought back to what Liz had said about the rally, and the fact that one of the antis had gone missing. A brash, very pretty woman, called Babette. A woman who Liz reckoned was a male-magnet. "One thing was quite strange though," I told Ben and Tanya. "During the rally today, Babette disappeared."

"What? As in poof?"

"Seems like it. And she hasn't been located yet. Maybe we should start our investigation by tracking down the missing Babette."

"And how do we do that?" asked Tanya. "If she disappeared in the middle of a rally she could be anywhere. How do we go about finding her?"

"I know where her parents live. Snuck a peek at Liz's log-book. She has some interesting details in there."

"I remember Babette." Ben gave a snort. Probably remembering Babette's standard attire of micro-minis two sizes too small, worn with high fuck-me shoes. "The woman's in her late thirties. Doubt you're gonna find her at her parent's house. More likely to be shacked up with some guy."

"But it's a starting point, Ben." I scowled at the phone. "And how come you remember Babette so well?"

"Um…no reason."

I snorted in disbelief, but left that conversation for another day. "Maybe her parents know which guy she's shacked up with and can point us in his direction."

"Be careful," Ben warned. "Have someone with you to watch ya back, don't take any unnecessary risks, and most of all…keep me in the loop. Ring before you go anywhere. Okay?"

"Okay?" He was so sweet. I could lick him all over, even without chocolate sauce.

"And don't forget you owe me a selfie before you hit the pillow tonight."

I felt a grin tugging at the corner of my mouth. "With or without my sunglasses?"

"Ooh, with…" He groaned. "When you wear nothing but those big bad sunglasses it makes me want to…"

"Enough!" yelled Tanya, grabbing another bottle of beer. "I'm still here, you know, guys."

"Later," I whispered into the phone. "Love you." And then I switched my phone off. Plenty of time for pillow-talk when I opened my front door, climbed the stairs, locked my bedroom door and began a fully videotaped, very slow, strip-tease.

And then, I thought of Ma, on a hard bed in a jail cell instead of sleeping in my bedroom tonight. Probably with a couple of drunks and a rapist for company. I let out a sigh. This gruesome image was enough to send my sexy thoughts plunging into a deep abyss, where they stayed.

I finished the bottle of beer in one long swig and climbed to my feet. "Better go, Tan. Can I count on your company after work tomorrow?"

"Yeah, okay. My lazy good-for-nothing ex is out of work at the moment. What's new? He can pick Erin up after school and look after her tomorrow night."

"Good. So, our first mission is to go look for Babette. And if she's at her parent's house, we'll find out what she knows."

I stood up and stretched. The moment I moved away from the big green armchair, Sweetie, who'd been glaring at me for the last half hour, leapt into the chair, spat in my direction, turned around three times and went to sleep.

Guess she was telling me who *really* owned that chair.

8

THE OUTSIDE OF THE CITY WATCH HOUSE, with its stark red bricks and vibes more depressing than a neglected cemetery, reared up out of the stone pavement in front of me. There was a coldness about the building that chilled my bones through to the marrow. What sort of night must my mother have endured inside those hostile red walls?

Guess I'd soon find out.

I'd talked Liz into accompanying me in return for a night out for her and Scott—my treat—at *Healthy Options* a newly opened vegetarian restaurant in Salisbury. What was it with these antis? They showed more compassion for a termite-infested tree than a member of their own family. Admittedly, a member who'd virtually wiped her youngest daughter from her memory banks over the last five years.

Even so, it was hard to believe my mother was a murder suspect. It didn't seem real. Fair enough, she was bossy and a lousy hugger…but a murderer? No way.

With these thoughts still swimming around in my head and close to drowning, I shoved against the front door of the long dark building topped by razor wire and stepped inside.

The prison smell hit me like a punch in the nose. Why is it that all institutions have their own distinctive smell? Hospitals reek of sickness and disinfectant. Aged care facilities of incontinence and stronger disinfectant. And prisons of sweat, body odor, and bottled rage.

"Who's in charge?" I asked the uniform behind the desk. "I would like to speak to whoever's in charge."

"Name please?"

"Katrina McKinley. And this is my sister, Elizabeth McKinley. A detective by the name of D.I. Adams arrested my mother last night and we're here to check on her and ensure she has employed the services of a good criminal lawyer."

A man in a baggy suit that looked as if it had been purchased at the Op shop that morning stepped into the room. Detective Inspector Garry Adams. "Ah, good morning, Ms. McKinley. Lovely to see you and your charming sister again," he said, his gravelly, trying-to-give-up-smoking-but-not-quite-succeeding voice scratching on my ears. "I hope you've come with new evidence, or at least a half-decent lawyer. The guy who is representing your mother is a first class imbecile. He thought your mother being in jail was a huge joke and kept falling over laughing. I wouldn't be surprised if he got his lawyer's degree from the back of a cereal box." He shook his head as though in pain. "If you know *anything* that will get your mother out of jail I'll personally shout you a drink. She's driving us insane."

I blinked. So it wasn't just her two daughters who had trouble getting along with Helen McKinley aka Queen Boadicea. It was the entire Universe. "Don't forget it was your bad, Detective," I told him. "You were the one who arrested my mother on the flimsy evidence of a bit of name-calling."

He sent a sideways glare at the now-grinning young constable behind the desk and then caught me in his headlights. "Name-calling, Ms. McKinley?" He slowly shook his head. "No, I'd classify, dirty rotten dog, as name-calling. Threatening to bash someone over the head hard enough to permanently switch off their lights, I'd call that pretty substantial evidence. Especially after finding that same *someone* with their head caved in."

Liz leant one elbow on the front desk and yawned as though bored with the whole conversation. "Who'd the old bag dig up for a lawyer?"

I scowled at her. There was no need to disrespect Ma in public. She scowled back at me. "Well, it's a wonder there was a lawyer left in the state who'd represent her," she said. "The woman's upset so many of them over the years."

DI Adams cleared his throat. "I believe the lawyer's name is Anthony Hamilton Jr."

"Uncle Tony?" Liz let out a yell and punched the air with her fist. "Ma's hired her kid brother to defend her." She looked across at me, her face crinkled in a Cheshire Cat grin. "Oh, my, God, let's go to the nearest pub and celebrate. My toffee-nosed mother will be in prison for the next thirty years."

I swallowed a laugh and almost choked on it. Liz was spot on. Our uncle was a white-collar lawyer—not a criminal lawyer. And even in that category he'd barely won a case in the last two years. I was inclined to agree with DI Adams' theory. Anthony Hamilton Jr., aka Uncle Tony, most likely cut out his lawyer degree from the back of a cereal box.

D.I. Adams scratched his head and his voice turned into a near-whisper. "So, if I can figure out a reason to turf him out for impropriety next time he comes in, any chance you can find a real criminal lawyer to represent your mother?"

I hesitated. Nodded. Surely there was *someone* out there in Lawyer-Land who hadn't heard of Helen McKinley. *Someone* who wouldn't go running for the hills the moment they heard her name. Ma had sued so many people, including her lawyers, over the years I didn't hold out much hope.

Liz was more optimistic. "Hey, all we gotta do is open the Yellow Pages of the phone-book at Lawyers and Other Money-Rip-Offs, close our eyes, stick a pin into the page and presto, we'll find a better lawyer than our Uncle Toby. I can't believe he's even agreed to represent Ma. Firstly, he doesn't know a thing about criminal law, and secondly, he hasn't been sober since his fortieth birthday."

"Any chance of seeing Ma?" I asked.

"Sorry, no visitors for prisoners at the Watch House, I'm afraid." DI

Adams shook his head. "Only lawyers."

"I could always dress up as a lawyer and…"

"No." DI Adam's looked down his nose at me but there was a definite twinkle in his eyes.

"So, we can't see her? Good!" Liz was already half way to the door. "That means instead of puking at the sight of Mother McKinley's supercilious sneer, we'll have time to try out a couple of super-food drinks at the New Age Juice Stand near the train station before we go home. Might even have time to check out the condition of the termites inside the marked-for-oblivion gum tree in the parklands."

I sighed. Followed my sister out the door. This could be another long day.

*****

Liz and I hadn't spent quality time together for quite a few years, so I reluctantly succumbed to squandering the rest of my precious morning participating in wacky hippie-type stuff with her. Such as drinking weird colored juice that looked and tasted like something you'd normally scoop out of a tadpole-polluted pond. Such as traipsing around the parklands, inspecting termite holes in trees and making sure the occupants were warm and toasty and well-fed. Such as marching and waving a banner while picketing the gates of a caged-hen egg factory.

After four hours of living in Liz's crazy anti-world, I was so relieved to turn my back on its wackiness, I sang along with my headphones all the way to the car. Hey, I couldn't wait to see that beloved sign over my front gate, *McKinley Greyhound Kennels*—couldn't wait to get home to my normal everyday life—even if my everyday life at the moment did contain a murderer. A murderer who'd callously framed my mother for his or her evil deed.

"You know, I never did find out how Ma ended up stoned." I turned my head to check on the silent Liz as we drove through Virginia on our last mile home. She was awake, so I continued. "Did Tinkerbelle trick Ma into eating her home-baked cookies? Or did Ma find the cookies hidden in the kitchen, think they were plain ordinary everyday cookies and have a couple of handfuls with her cup of tea? Or was it something more sinister? What about the stew Ma was cooking on the stove? Maybe someone dosed the stew with some very questionable drug, while she wasn't looking. And maybe, if we can find out who purposely sent Ma on a trip into Ga-Ga Land, principally so she wouldn't see or hear them battering Tinkerbelle over the head with a shovel and burying her body in the sand, we'll have our murderer."

"Yeah…maybe." Liz didn't sound overly enthused.

"So, the moment we arrive home, you can help me pull the kitchen apart looking for a clue. Luckily, I potted Ma's stew and refrigerated it. Easy enough to scoop out a sample and send it off to have it tested."

Liz stretched her arms straight in the air, clasped her fingers together and clicked her head from side to side in the archway formed. Either loosening the kinks or performing some bizarre ritual that all hippies undergo when they get close to home base. "Surely," she said while continuing to turn her head from side to side, "if there was something to find in your kitchen, the police would have already found it."

"Not necessarily. We know what we're looking for. The police don't."

Liz set her head-rolling exercise on pause and rolled her eyes at me. "And what is it we're looking for?"

I frowned. Shook my head. "I don't know, do I? Well, not literally…"

"I rest my case." Liz continued her head-turning, much more slowly this time. She breathed in through her nose when she turned her head to the left and out through her mouth when she turned her head to the right.

Disregarding Liz's skepticism, I drove on, eager to arrive home and begin my investigation. I'd know it was a clue when I found it. Just wasn't sure, at this stage, exactly what 'it' might be.

I also knew, the moment we pulled up outside my front gate, that my plan may be in jeopardy. There was a large printed sign propped up against the gate: FOR THOSE IN NEED—PLEASE TAKE ONE. Two big bulging garbage bags lay side by side next to the printed sign. One bag had come open and a horse statue that used to reside on a shelf in my lounge room, plus a pair of my knee-less jeans, poked out the top. An old guy dressed in a suit and tie, who looked far from being 'in need', waved to us as he drove off in his shiny blue utility. Six big bulging garbage bags piled in the back.

9

I was going to kill someone and join my mother in jail for the next twenty years.

There was no other way around it. While I'd been away from home, playing reluctant anti-protest-games with my darling sister, her deranged friends had entered my house and performed weird rituals. Weird rituals that included throwing away half my stuff and moving my furniture around. In an attempt to curtail my murderous thoughts, I took a deep breath, held it for ten, and then slowly let it out to the count of ten. Hopefully, if I remained calm, the world would go back to spinning on its axis, and life would become normal again. No such luck—even though I counted to ten so slowly I almost carked it when I ran out of breath.

In desperation, I ground my teeth together until they ached. I fisted my hands by my sides, nails cutting deep into my palms.

Nothing helped.

Out of the corner of my eye I spotted Liz sneaking through the front door. She took one quick glance around, grinned broadly, and then scurried up the stairs. I heard the guest room door slam behind her and the bolt slide into its socket.

No help there either.

While we were away, my sister's daft friends had transformed my house. They'd potted trails of green herbs into planters and lined them up just inside my front door—perfect for Tater to cock his leg and water several times a day. They'd sprinkled the carpet in the passage with some vile smelling white ash. And when I walked into the kitchen, holding my breath, I let out a scream of frustration. They'd pushed my kitchen table up next to the open window, stood my kitchen chairs in a row outside the window in the dirt, and all the jars of spices and sauces lined up on the top shelf had disappeared.

I let out another scream, loud enough to be heard at the Two Wells Pizza shop, three miles away. "What in blazes have you done to my beautiful house?"

"We're decluttering, Katrina," said Mystique in a matte-of-fact voice as she floated through the doorway dressed in a peasant blouse, long flowing multicolored skirt, and those awful Birkenstock sandals protesters insist on wearing, without socks, which reveal just how rarely they wash their feet. "Feng Shui, darling. We're eliminating all the negative energy that's built up since your demented mother murdered our Tinkerbelle."

I rammed my itching fingers deep inside my coat pockets to prevent them from wrapping around the woman's long elegant neck. "My mother did *not* murder Tinkerbelle!"

Mystique, and her twin sister, Spirit, were fruitcakes of the highest order. And it looked like they'd been the ones tearing my house apart while I was away. And then I thought, maybe my devious sister was behind all this mumbo jumbo. Maybe Liz purposely kept me away for four hours? Maybe she'd arranged for the mystical twins to do a job on my house today? But why?

"We're trying to help you, Katrina," Mystique insisted. "Your house was in need of spiritual cleansing. In fact, your whole karmic cycle was out of whack. Because of this terrible murder, evil lurked in every corner of your house, ready and willing to inflict more bad juju. My sister, Spirit, and I have cleansed your home with Feng Shui which has allowed the good energy to flow again."

"Feng Shui? Feng Fooey!" I shouted at her. "You two cretins threw all my stuff away! I can't believe your stupidity. How could you think for one minute that it was okay to discard anything of mine without asking me?" I was so angry I wanted to jump up and down and scream and kick and throw a terrible-two tantrum. But I didn't. I was very mature and restrained. I merely stamped my foot so hard it felt like I'd broken a toe. "Okay, now you can go find the guy with the blue ute who grabbed six bags of my belongings and get them all back."

"Can't do that, Kat," sang Spirit, as she followed her sister, Mystique, out of the lounge room, bunches of what looked like dried lavender nests in each hand. Swirling smoke, stinking like Scott's nose-curling socks, emanated from the stalks. And what made it worse, Spirit methodically waved the stuff in circles, chanting and spreading the smoke everywhere she went.

"What the hell are doing now?" I roared at her, my breath caught up in my throat. "Cleansing the negative energy by burning my house to the ground?"

"I'm smudging with dried sage," Spirit crooned, her smile serene and securely glued into place. "I'm purifying your house by eradicating dark negative energy and calling up the good energy. It's an ancient cleansing ritual, well known in Native American folk lore, Katrina. First we de-cluttered, then repositioned the furniture and now all that's left is the smudging. After that, your house will be bright and cheerful and free of evil once again."

Spirit, still waving the smoking stalks in circles, moved toward me. "Good spirits stay," she chanted, sending the smoke into my eyes and mouth and making me cough. "Bad spirits go away and never return."

A whimper from the lounge room alerted me to the dogs. My heart catapulted down to my toes and then bounced back up into my throat. "What have you done with my dogs? If you've decluttered or smudged or hurt Tater and Lucky in any way, I'll toss you both out on your skinny backsides and you can pitch your tents and do your wacky woo-woo stuff in the middle of the roadway."

Not waiting for confirmation either way, I raced into the lounge room. And came to a skidding halt. My mouth opened. I blinked. This wasn't *my* lounge room. Nothing was where it should be. My statues had disappeared off the shelves and been replaced by a jungle of green plants. The lounge chairs were in a different place. My three-seated settee blocked the other doorway, the one that led into the kitchen. And my racing trophies? Where were my racing trophies?

Lucky slunk out from behind one of the lounge chairs, a woeful, 'Please-Mum-I-didn't-do-it', look on her face. I bent down and hugged her to me, then rubbed behind her ears. "Why didn't you bite them?" I whispered in her ear. She licked her lips as if to say, 'I wanted to but couldn't find you to ask if it was okay,' and then she eyed the smoke in the room from under her eyelids, shook her head and sneezed.

I rubbed one hand over the top of her head and peered over my shoulder. No small tan-colored Chihuahua striding importantly around the room, or bouncing up and down ready to take on an army. "Where's my other dog?" I yelled so the two dingbats smudging the passageway could hear me. "What have you done with Tater?"

Mystique popped her head around the corner of the door. "Sorry Katrina, we had to put him outside. He kept grabbing at the bottom of my skirt and shaking it."

I lifted one eyebrow at her. Good boy, Tater.

Spirit slid into the room, still madly waving her smoky stalks, although I was glad to hear her cough behind her hand before she cleared her throat and spoke. "Unfortunately, that little dog of yours emits bad energy," she said.

"Bad energy?" I repeated in a voice loud enough to lift the ceiling.

"Yes. He kept humping my leg."

"And?" I narrowed my eyes at her but she was too deep in her weird mumbo jumbo world to catch my warning.

"If it had been up to me, I'd have stuffed the bad juju-dog in one of the garbage bags with the rest of your junk, but my sister wouldn't let me. Instead, we shooed him outside. Had to throw a bucket of holy water over him a couple of times because he wouldn't stop barking. His noise was interfering with the Feng Shui."

Fury, slowly building inside me, spewed forth in one angry shout. "Arrrrgggggg…" These two mad, Birkenstop-sandaled hippies had contemplated stuffing my gorgeous, twinkly-eyed Tater in a garbage bag along with the rest of my belongings and placing him outside the front gate to be given away. These two cracked, crazy critters had deliberately chucked a bucket of water over my fierce warrior dog. My tiny Chihuahua who thought he was a Doberman. Cursing wildly, I stomped to the back door, threw it open and let a wet, bug-eyed, Tater inside.

He shook himself, grinned up at me and took off, his tail standing stiff in the air.

"Sic 'em, Tater!" I shouted and took off after him, with Lucky cantering beside me. "Show 'em what we think of crazies who trash people's houses and bad-mouth their dogs."

Spirit, mouth open in a piercing squeal, dropped the sage sticks on the floor. Mystique grabbed a handful of her long dirndl skirt and lifted it high in the air. And then they both sprinted like a couple of race horses for the front door.

"Don't let him bite me!" Spirit howled as she flew along the passageway, Tater barking at her heels. "We were only trying to help."

"It's your fault," growled Mystique as she shoved her sister out the way so she could throw herself through the front door first. "I told you Kat was sensitive about her animals. But would you listen? Oh no. You read up on that silly smudging thing online and thought you knew it all."

"In a hurry, ladies?" It was DI Adams, his arms spread in an attempt to stay upright as the Woo-Woo twins barged through the doorway, almost bulldozing him to the ground. They didn't stop. Didn't apologize for crashing into him. Just kept running until they reached their tent on the far side of the lawn.

I whistled for Tater and he came strutting back to me, eyes bright, his cheeky grin reminding me of that naughty gremlin in the movie of the same name.

"You scaring the residents of Tent City?" the detective asked, his eyebrows raised in query.

"More like the other way around," I growled as I picked Tater up and cuddled him to me. "D'ya know anything about Feng Shui, or Smudging?"

He shook his head in confusion. "Can't say I do."

"Well, I advise you not to let those two idiots near your house or you'll lose half your belongings." I took a step to the side to give the detective room to get past. "Want to come inside and fill me in on your bad news while I make us a cup of coffee? Whenever a policeman arrives at the front door, it's rarely to impart good news." I led the way into the kitchen, filled the kettle with water and put it on the stove to boil. "Has something happened to Ma? Did she get into a fight with another prisoner? Spit at one of the guards?"

"No, nothing like that." He shook his head and then shrugged one shoulder. "Although she's on a hunger strike at the moment and demanding we provide her with needle and thread so she can sew her lips together." He rolled his eyes heavenward. "Honestly, I'm tempted to help her thread the needle. Be worth the paper-work just to shut her up for a while. But, no, I was outside checking the crime scene and thought I'd pop in and let you in on the latest developments."

I felt my mouth spring open into fly-catching mode. "You did?"

"Well, you actually helped solve the murders in those other cases you found yourself involved in. Even if you *did* come close to getting killed yourself, both times." His words made me grow a couple of inches taller. D.I. Adams, who'd up until now treated me like I was a loose cannon, actually appreciated my help. I grinned up at him. "However," he went on. "The bad news is that forensics found blood on your mother's clothes. *And* it was Tinkerbelle's blood."

That took the smile off my face. "Could have been from a bloody nose."

'Yes, I know, but it's another point against her. Especially as at the moment your mother is our only suspect." He reached for two coffee mugs, placed a spoonful of Nescafe in each. Seemed quite happy to make himself at home in my kitchen. "By the way, have you and your sister found her another lawyer yet? We ditched your Uncle Tony this morning after he rolled into the precinct stinking drunk, fell over a crack in the tiles and as he went down, he reached out for the nearest desk, dragging our computer system onto the ground with him."

"That sounds like our Uncle Tony," I said pouring hot water into the two mugs. "The good news is Liz spoke to the anti's lawyer at the rally today and he promised to take Ma on. George Hudson. Heard of him?"

"Yeah. He'll do. The professional protestors' friend. We arrest them and George gets them out within the hour. Just like a revolving door." He picked up his coffee and placed it on the table then looked around the kitchen for a chair.

"The chairs are out in the garden," I told him pointing through the window. "Courtesy of Dumb and Dumber. We either take our coffee into the garden or bring the chairs back in here. Your choice. But first, if I give you a sample of the stew Ma cooked yesterday, could you get it tested for drugs? Someone got Ma stoned while I was at the Gawler track and I'm thinking it was the killer. Why else would they send her on a drug-fueled trip, unless they wanted her out of the way while they bumped off Tinkerbelle? And I'm also thinking, whatever they used to get her off her face may have been slipped into the stew Ma was cooking."

"Good point," said DI Adams, ears pricked. "I'll take a sample with me and see what we can find."

"Thank you. That'd be great. If we can prove Ma's stew was drugged it would be evidence that she was also a victim and not a suspect." I opened the refrigerator door, peered inside and swore, loudly. "I'm going to kill 'em!" I growled through gritted teeth. All that was left on the refrigerator shelves was a dried-up pickle, three tomatoes, a bottle of water, and a skunky lemon. The rest of my food was gone. De-cluttered. "I'm going to set fire to them, throw them over a cliff and then push a boulder over the edge so it squashes them flat...and *then* I'll kill 'em."

"What's wrong?"

"The Woo-Woo twins have decluttered my refrigerator—thrown my food out because it created bad energy." I paused for effect. "And that includes Ma's stew."

10

Aₙ ʜᴏᴜʀ ʟᴀᴛᴇʀ, I ᴅʀᴏᴠᴇ ᴍʏ sᴛᴀᴛɪᴏɴ ᴡᴀɢᴏɴ along the Northern Expressway toward the beach-side town of Semaphore. The showers, which had been sporadic all morning, had now developed into a downpour.

"So, what did DI Adams do?" asked Tanya who sat beside me, rapidly emptying a jumbo-sized bag of sour cream and chives potato chips.

"What *could* he do?" I shrugged one shoulder. "The food they'd thrown out was way past being rescued. And when DI Adams questioned the twins about Ma's stew, Spirit said the stuff emanated evil vibes so she'd tipped it down the drain. A bit dodgy, I thought. It meant Ma's stew couldn't be tested for drugs. Got me wondering. They're identical twins, so maybe one stayed at the rally, pretending to be both, while the other twin came back, got Ma stoned, and then belted Tinkerbelle over the head."

"But why?"

"Well, when the cops interviewed them, they said they adored the deceased, but they didn't. Not really. Tinkerbelle was always putting them down and calling them bad names. How could you adore someone like that?"

Tanya tipped the now-empty bag upside down and caught the remaining chip, which she transferred to her mouth. "You know," she said, between chews. "I did witness The Wicked Witch slamming Spirit up against the house, once."

"Yeah? When?"

"One day last week. I was pulling up outside your gate when I heard Tinkerbelle screaming and ranting at Spirit. Heard the supposed Earth Mother threatening to cut off Spirit's hands if she ever touched her things again."

"Probably got caught decluttering Tinkerbelle's tent."

No sympathy there.

As we drove over the steel-girded bridge spanning the Port River, I peered through the rain at the colorful boats bobbing in the water below. "Something else has been bothering me," I said and glanced across at my friend. "Spirit accused me of being a hypocrite. Reckons I claim to love animals, yet I'll make a meal out of a dead animal." I shook my head, the thought still worrying me. "Okay, I consider cows are quite cute, and sweet, but I also enjoy sinking my teeth into a nice tender piece of T-bone steak covered in Dianne sauce." I raised my eyebrows at Tanya. "So, Tan, does that make me a bad person?"

Tanya, evidently trying not to laugh, let out a muffled snort. "No, of course not. It just makes you slightly dysfunctional in a house-full of whackos."

"Thank you. I think." I turned from the Expressway onto Victoria Road and then across onto Semaphore Road. "Anyway, today, I got so angry with Spirit, if Adams hadn't been standing there eying me off like he was just waiting for an excuse to handcuff me, I'd have tossed the ditzy blonde into the garbage bin along with my discarded food, and then nailed the lid down tight."

"Shame I wasn't there. I'd have distracted your scruffy detective friend and then held the lid down while you hammered in the nails."

I grinned across at Tanya, grateful warmth filling my chest. Talk about a loyal friend. Tanya was always there for me. Always ready to lend a hand, no matter the consequences. "I tried to get Mystique and Spirit arrested for disposing of the evidence," I told her. "But Adams didn't see it my way."

"He never does,' said Tanya

"That's exactly what I told him but he didn't respond. Merely finished drinking his coffee, shook his head at me again and shuffled out the door mumbling something about like mother like daughter."

"Must be getting close to Babette's parents' shop," said Tanya as we drove slowly down Semaphore Road, past the TAB, squinting through the rain at the numbers on houses and shops. A popular little suburb set on the beach-front, Semaphore boasted rows of old-world specialty shops that lined both sides of the road.

Still squinting, I pulled up at the traffic lights and quickened the windscreen wipers. "That looks like number 42," I said, pointing to an Indian restaurant on the corner. "So Babette's parents must own the shop next door."

"It's an antique shop."

The lights changed to green so I drove across the road and angled into a vacant parking space in front of *Old Timers*, a run-down, double-fronted shop that looked older than the goods on sale. "I love browsing through antique shops," I told Tanya. "You sometimes find the most unusual items. I remember once I found a book about greyhounds that was written back in the early 1900's, way before track-racing started, when the South Australian colonists rode their horses out hunting and used greyhounds to chase kangaroos and wallabies. Of course there were no rabbits and hares in Australia at that time. The land-owners introduced them later."

"And regretted it ever since."

"Hey, look at those old toy buses," I said, swinging my body out of the car and hurrying to shelter from the rain under the shop front. "I can just imagine some rich kid playing with those, like a hundred years ago." Out the front of the shop were three large colorful toy buses. They'd been wheeled into the middle of the footpath for all passers-by to see and exclaim over. The toy buses were scratched, battered and made of lead, but quite interesting, in an I-wonder-how-old-they-are sort of way. I bent down and flicked over the price tag. Oh My God. $1,200. I dropped the tag like it was a large furry spider and walked into the shop.

There were only two people browsing the merchandise. I ran an eye over the woman serving behind the counter. In her early-sixties, thin wispy hair dyed purple with blonde streaks, face layered with makeup, and dressed like a gypsy dancer. So…this was Babette's mother. As they say, acorns don't fall far from the tree. Funny thing though, this woman had the sort of face that invited you to tell her your life story. She'd be a good listener under her airy-fairy exterior. I checked to see if she had a crystal ball. None on show—but that didn't mean there wasn't one tucked under the counter.

She'd finished wrapping the purchased item and handed it to the young woman with a smile. "That milk-maid statue will look fab in your mum's living room, Katy," the woman said, handing the wrapped parcel to her customer. "She's already bought a shepherd tending a little lamb statue. They'll go well together."

When the customer moved away from the counter, I stepped forward. "Hello, Mrs. Germaine. I'm Kat McKinley and this is my friend, Tanya Ashford. I rang this morning about your daughter, Babette."

"Please, call me Delphine." She let out sigh and shook her head. "I'm afraid one day it will be the Gods from Heaven who visit me in the middle of the night, all dressed in their ethereal beauty, informing me my only daughter was taken up to the Pearly Gates, but refused entry. My Babette never rings home any more. We see her only when she wants money. And each time she's with a different man, most who appear as though they've recently been released from prison." She clasped her hands under her chin. "And the men's auras? Oh, dear. Always so black, so intense, it hurts my eyes. And my heart." She moved from behind the counter and beckoned for us to follow her. "Come, I will show you a picture of my Babette that will tear your heart apart. So beautiful. So precious. My Babette was a sweet angel before she left our protection and moved into a world of hate and violence."

Delphine led us toward the back of the shop, stopping on the way to inform a tall thin guy with a beard so long he could use it as a scarf on a cold day, that she was taking a break and to keep an eye out for customers.

"Your husband?" I asked as I followed her into a little kitchen.

"No, my husband's out at the moment. Gone to look at a consignment from a deceased estate. That was my brother, Jonah. He helps out three days a week."

Delphine reached inside a cupboard and removed three framed photographs. Lovingly, she set them down on top of a badly scratched antique desk, advertised for sale at a you'll-never-find-a-mug-silly-enough-to-buy-this price of $15,000. I watched her closely. Outwardly the woman was showing little emotion other than love for the little girl she'd lost to the outside world. But I could see, deep down, she was worried. About what? Her missing daughter? Or what her missing daughter could have done before she went missing?

"This is my darling Babette at the age of one, seven, and thirteen," she told us, pointing to each of the three photographs. Tanya and I bent get a closer look. Geez. This kid either had a penchant for *fairies*, or her dotty mother enjoyed dressing her up. While the earlier photos were cute and showed a happy little girl with a mile-wide smile, the photo of thirteen-year old Babette, showed a smoldering rebel. An angry teenager dressed in a tutu with fairy wings. She was scowling at the camera, like she had an axe hidden under her tutu and if she got half a chance whoever was behind the camera might find the axe embedded in their skull.

I could see Delphine stoking the fires ready to tell us more sickly-sweet stories about her long-ago baby Babette. I cleared my throat. Had to get the elephant in the room out in the open, or we'd spend the next half hour discussing Babette's sheltered childhood and learn nothing of today's angry woman. "Your daughter has been camping on my lawn for the last month with several other protesters," I broke in. "One of them, Tinkerbelle, was killed yesterday. Murdered. Would your Babette be capable of murder, Delphine?"

That stopped her. She frowned, picked up the three photographs as though they were embossed with gold and carefully slid them back into the cupboard. "I think we're *all* capable of murder, Ms. McKinley. That is, if we're put into a life-threatening situation." Oh dear, now we were back to formal names. "Imagine if someone threatened you. Wouldn't you snatch up a carving knife, stick the knife so deeply into the attacker's chest that it came out through his back, and then wriggle the knife around in the wound to create more excruciating pain? Wouldn't you then stomp on the attacker's face with a pair of football boots until blood spurted out of both eyes? And then, to make sure the attacker didn't get up and run away, wouldn't you grab your gun and shoot him in both knees?"

Yikes!

I took two steps backwards, glanced across at Tanya and caught her retreating too.

"But, no," Delphine continued, "I don't think my Babette would set out to willingly take the life of another human being." She turned to look me full in the eye and I blanched at the menace. "But some of those thugs and losers she hooks up with would happily snuff someone out for a reason as benign as snoring and keeping them awake at night."

"Um…do you know who your daughter is in a relationship with at the moment?"

"No, only that he's the husband of one of the other protesters."

"What? She's having it off with one of the protester's husbands?" Tanya's voice rose. Like me, her ears were flapping at this bit of news. "Who? Whose husband?"

"She didn't say. Didn't introduce him to us."

Damn. That would have been a valuable clue. I've often wondered where the protesters' husbands and partners lived. Except for Scott, who rarely left his bed, the protesters were all women. The men were probably at home looking after the kids.

"He was a bad egg, that last one," Delphine continued. "When Babette brought him here a month ago, he stole money from our till. Noah, my brother, demanded he put the money back or he'd ring the police. And do you know what this man my daughter brought home did to Noah? He broke his nose. Told us if anyone went within five hundred yards of a policeman he'd come back and break every bone in Noah's body and then chop him into bite size pieces and feed him to the sharks."

Double yikes!

"Maybe he had something to do with the murder," put in Tanya.

"Maybe. How did this Tinkerbelle woman die?" asked Delphine.

"Bludgeoned to death with a shovel and buried under a pile of sand on my property," I said. "It was awful. I found her. And the police arrested my mother for the woman's murder. My mother didn't do it. She was framed. That's why Tanya and I are investigating. We're trying to clear Ma's name."

"And the Gods are smiling down on you for being such a good daughter." Delphine smiled and the airy-fairy gypsy had returned. Thank God. The other Delphine, the woman with unorthodox ways of doing away with people, was freakingly scary. Delphine's smile widened. "Your mother must be so proud of you."

I glanced across at Tanya who ran a hand across her mouth and snorted. Either the smell of garlic emanating from the half-eaten sandwich sitting on top of the $15,000 antique desk was affecting her sinuses or she was laughing behind her hand at the thought of my mother ever being proud of me.

Delphine lifted a hideous statue of what could only be described as a dog with evil goblin genes out of a cardboard box and settled it beside the cigarette stand. "So, is there anything else you want to know about my Babette?"

"Any idea where she could be now?"

"None at all, I'm afraid. Last I heard she was camping on someone's front lawn."

"Yeah, that'd be *my* lawn. And she's not there now. Disappeared during a protest-march in town, yesterday."

"I'm sorry I can't help you," said Delphine and looked as though she really meant it. "But if you do catch up with her, will you tell her that her mother is worried about her and to call home. She can reverse the charges."

I sighed. Guess it must be hard being a mum. Even if your kids are all grown-up and shifted to the dark side. "Okay," I said, moving toward the front door. "And thanks for talking to us, Delphine. You've been a great help."

Resisting the temptation to surf through a shelf full of tattered old books near the front of the shop, I followed Tanya through the front door and out onto the footpath.

"Hang on," called out Delphine from behind us. "I just remembered something. Babette did say the piece-of-shit guy she was living with had a house in Wild Horse Plains. Maybe she decided to ditch her protester friends and go shack up with him." She shook her head. "All I can say is, if she has, God help her."

11

I was running late. *Really* late …

So, when Tanya leaped from the car to open the front gate, the noise emanating from my racing kennels sounded like the last minutes of a football Grand Final. Every dog on the property was voicing its displeasure at my tardiness. While Tanya waited until I drove through the gate, then closed it again, I glanced across at the GAP kennels. Yeah. Even Yolo and Ralph had joined in the fun. I rolled my eyes at them as they yapped, bounced and twisted in the mud, like a couple of just-lit, firecrackers.

When Tanya offered to help with the dogs, naturally I took her up on the offer. Sent her inside the house to feed Lucky and Tater, give them lots of hugs and then let them out into the backyard. Hey, if everyone had a friend like Tanya, more people in the world would have reason to smile.

After changing into my rubber boots on the front porch, I hurried along the path that led to the kennel-house. Cat, the undomesticated feline who resided under the wood pile, continually teased my dogs, and acted like she paid the mortgage on my property, stalked across the path in front of me. Probably off to catch a couple of mice to feed her babies. I drew in a deep breath and let it out slowly. The dampness in the air smelled earthy, fresh. The sky, although still overcast, had white patches pushing through the gray. In fact, I could feel a bounce, a spring in my step—until I reached the spot where I'd found Tinkerbelle.

My feet faltered and then refused to move.

I stood in front of the crime scene tape, arms wrapped around my stomach, an icy coldness seeping into my chest. Seemed like I couldn't go past that sand pile without experiencing the same abject horror I'd felt on discovering a dead tattooed arm adorned with colored bracelets, poking out from under the sand.

It could have been one minute—or ten—but that's where Jake, returning for late-afternoon duties, found me.

Jake hopped off his bike and ambled over to stand beside me. "Hey, Kat."

I shook myself. Cleared my head, but didn't dispel the overall numbness. "Howdy Jake," I said, voice a bit wobbly. "Sorry, I haven't started the dogs yet."

"No worries, man." Jake pulled at one of his nose rings and like me, stared at the sand pile. "Guess this means like, the workmen won't be doing any work today or tomorrow."

"Or the next day…" I sighed and forced my legs to move, to walk away from the crime scene. "Police questioned you yet?"

"Yeah." Jake, wheeling his bike, slouched along beside me. "That grumpy cop with the lousy dress-sense, he sort-of invited himself into my pad last night."

Lousy dress sense? If this wasn't so serious I'd crack up laughing. My dreadlocked kennel-assistant was currently wearing pink tracksuit pants, a bilious green polar neck jumper and an orange beanie. Instead, I kept the grin hidden. "And what did DI Adams want to know?"

"Like, when I'd last seen Tinkerbelle."

"Fair enough."

Jake wrinkled his nose. "*And* if I, like, heard your Ma and Tinkerbelle fighting."

"Damn. And I had you listening in and reporting to me, so of course you heard every loud, ear-splitting word." I frowned at him. "But Tinkerbelle *was* still alive when you went home, wasn't she?"

"Scarily alive, man." The whites of Jake's eyes stood out and he shook his head. "Hell, dude, I thought it would be your Ma who ended up with chunks out of her head, not the wicked witch."

I swallowed the lump in my throat at the thought of how close I'd come to being an orphan and opened the kennel-house door. "Jake, do you think Tinkerbelle could have forced marijuana-laced cookies down Ma's throat? Or spiked the stew Ma was cooking? Or was there a stranger hiding out somewhere near the house? A stranger, who firstly took care of Ma and then took *extra* care of Tinkerbelle?" I frowned at my dude-helper. "Jake, did you see anyone other than Ma and Tinkerbelle hanging around before you left to go home?"

Jake leaned his bike up against the shed and shook his head.

"Anything at all out of the ordinary?"

"Nothing."

"Think carefully, Jake. The slightest thing could be important."

"Only person I saw was the boss-man delivering a load of sand. And that was after you came home. Your Ma was already higher than a kite by then."

"And Tinkerbelle was already dead," I added with a shiver. "She was hidden under a thin layer of sand and that truck driver buried the body completely, without realizing it."

"Why don't you ask your Ma where she scored the drugs?"

I slipped a lead around the neck of the greyhound in the first kennel, Lofty, and another on Suzy, the white and black bitch in the second kennel, and led them both to the door. "I would if I could," I told Jake as the dogs pulled me through the doorway. "But the police won't let me see her and she's not co-operating with them. She's refused to tell the police anything."

"Hey, dude, your Ma's a scary lady too. I screamed like a girl when she and Tinkerbelle ogled me through the window. They were snarling and white frothy stuff, like, spewed outta their mouths. Oh boy, they went crazy. And when a fry-pan and some sort of heavy rolling-pin thing smashed against the wall, I like, grabbed me bike and took off for home." He shook his head, eyes bugging wider. "No way was I hanging around waiting to be chopped up and added to your ma's stew."

I left Jake to sweep the kennels while I set Lofty and Suzy loose in one of the back paddocks. On the way back, I spotted Tanya walking along the path. "Hey, are the terrible two all sorted?"

"Yeah," she answered. "Tater wanted me to lift him up into the fridge so he could choose his own dinner, but I persuaded him that a tin of Turkey Dinner for Dogs was a way better option than the pathetic stuff you call food. Did you know your fridge contains three tomatoes, a dried-up pickle, a bottle of water, a skunky lemon, and what looked like a packet of something green that may or may not be alive? No way was I going to check it out."

"Thanks to the Declutter Sisters, that's all the food I have left," I told her. "I *was* going to dine on sausages, eggs and chips. Now, I guess I'll have to ring the Pizza Joint in Two Wells, if I want to eat. Unless I try a tin of Turkey Dinner for Dogs too."

While Jake and Tanya let the rest of the team out into the back paddocks and swept the kennels, I prepared twenty dog-dinners. Each high-quality beef and kibble meal, flavored with a mixture of Cup-a-Soup and hot water, sprinkled with raw carrot, and fortified with vitamins. Then, after shaking and straightening a couple of untidy dog blankets, I placed a meal in every kennel. A meal giving off such a tempting aroma, I almost grabbed a large spoon and helped myself.

Hmm…my dogs were getting choice beef for dinner, while I was settling for take-away pizza. Not sure what that said about the pecking order around here.

Racing team settled for the night, Jake fastened his helmet under his chin, waved to Tanya and me, and began wheeling his bike toward the front gate. Suddenly he stopped and spun around, his dreadlocks flying. "Hey dude," he called out in his little-boy voice, "sure you'll be, like, okay, without a man to, like, protect you tonight?"

Tanya slid me a glance that said she was trying hard not to crack up, while I covered my mouth with one hand. "No, no, you get off home,

Jake. I'll be fine. Liz's boyfriend, Scott, is in the house."

Jake frowned. "Yeah, man, but that Scott guy, he never gets out of bed."

"I'll be fine," I persisted. "I have my two guard dogs, Tater and Lucky, to look after me." I waved Jake on and watched as he opened and closed the front gate and then wobbled off down the road. "Even if Tater never bites…only humps," I added with a grin at Tanya, "and Lucky runs and hides in the lounge, behind the chair."

By the time we'd reached Tanya's car which was parked in front of the house, the protesters were out of their tents sitting around a camp fire eating whatever it was they'd cooked for tea. Smelt like bootlaces and boiled seaweed to me. Not much of a life, really, I thought. Couldn't understand why these women had to live like gypsies for their causes. Either they were fanatical about saving the environment—or just plain fanatical.

"Well, today wasn't a completely lost cause," said Tanya breaking into my thoughts. "We discovered Babette's latest boyfriend is the husband of one of that lot over there. *And* he lives near Wild Horse Plains. That's more than you knew this morning." She paused, lifted one eyebrow at me. "Thing is, are you going to do anything about it?"

"Well, it's the best clue I've had so far."

"Kat, it's your *only* clue"

I wrinkled my nose at her. "Okay. Okay. I'll check with Liz tonight. Find out who's married and who isn't and maybe dig up the address at Wild Horse Plains."

"Good move."

"And then it's just a matter of checking to see if Babette is with this guy and asking if either of them know anything about Tinkerbelle's murder."

"That's all?"

"Yep. I'll go tomorrow. And before you start…I'll carry a canister of pepper spray in my coat pocket."

"And maybe a couple of grenades in your tote-bag?"

I laughed. "Don't worry—I'll even take Lofty along for the ride. His shark teeth can be very off-putting to a stranger."

"Good idea. Can't be too careful. Remember, Babette's mum reckons this guy's really bad news, Kat. I'd come with you, but I have to work." She tipped her head to one side. "What about Liz?"

"Liz?" I shook my head. "Unless there's a tree that needs hugging or a beached whale that requires TLC, Elizabeth McKinley will be keeping her good-for-nothing boyfriend company all day tomorrow…in bed. It's a wonder that guy hasn't developed bed sores. He's been here a month and I reckon I've seen him three times. And when I do, he's dressed in nothing but socks and jocks and heading into or out of the bathroom."

"And the only exercise he gets is when he has animal sex with your sister?"

"Which, going by the noises emanating from my guest room, is on average, five times a day."

I opened the car door for Tanya and stepped back. "Anyway, don't worry about me. I'll be okay on my own. I can't see anyone giving me trouble with Lofty by my side. One look at his ugly face, his dinner-plate paws and the size of his canine teeth and they'll run screaming to their Mama."

"True." Tanya slid into the driving seat. "But I'd feel much happier if there was another human in the car too. Someone who could at least use a mobile phone to ring the police if you got into trouble. Can't see Lofty managing that."

"True," I agreed. "That's a trick I haven't taught him yet."

"Well, I'm off," said Tanya. "If I know Dan, he'll be watching the races on Sky-Channel while Erin plays non-stop video games. My lazy ex always leaves it to me to see our daughter does her homework." She turned the key in the ignition and cut me a worried glance. "And remember, you promised Ben you'd ring him. The poor guy worries about you. And please…ring me too. As soon as you get back safely. Okay?"

"Yes, Mum." I grinned. "And thanks for coming with me today to talk to Babette's mother."

"No worries. It's always a fascinating experience to tag along with you when you're in the middle of an investigation." She put the car in gear, preparing to move off. "At least this time we didn't stumble over any dead bodies."

*****

The sky was gunmetal grey, clouds were low, and night wasn't too far away. Shivering in the cold air, I wrapped my arms around my body and hurried inside. Where was Liz? I needed some questions answered so I could work out who Babette was hooked up with.

Persistent scratching at the back door interrupted my thoughts and brought me to a standstill. Tater let out a sharp bark. Then Lucky added a pathetic whine. Both clearly saying 'Hurry up, Mum. We haven't been for our walk yet.'

"Okay, guys. I'm sorry. I know I'm a bad Mum, but hey, it's been one of those days."

Tater's answering bark sounded more like a snort of disbelief as if to say, stop making piffling excuses woman, find our leads and let's get going.

"Your wish is my command," I told him and gave an exaggerated bow as he strutted past, short bossy tail stuck high in the air. Lucky followed, tongue lolling to one side in an open-mouthed grin.

Okay, it appeared quizzing my sister would have to wait until after I'd finished walking the dogs. I stuffed a woolen beanie on my head, attached leads to collars, and opened the front door. "So…which way do you want to go, tonight?"

Tater yanked me in the direction of the front gate, evidently eager to do some road walking, while Lucky opted for the back paddocks.

"Make up your minds, guys. I can't split myself in half."

Tater won the debate. Of course. He always won—which proves size doesn't always count. Tiny Tater thought he was a Stegosaurus, while Lucky, the ex-racing greyhound, knew she was just a squishy soft marshmallow.

With the two dogs on the end of the lead, I headed in the direction of the front gate, where I'd pick up the two GAP dogs and take them road-walking with us. Once my house and property was free of protesters, I'd be able to bring Yolo and Ralph inside, get them house-trained and ready for their adoptive parents and life after racing.

As we came closer to the front gate, which I always insisted be kept latched, I could see it was wide open. Strange. And outside the gate I could see two fair-haired children playing on the road. Jamie and Charlotte, Mary's children. The two-year old sat in the middle of a puddle blithely making mud pies and trying to eat them, while the four-year old appeared to be playing a noisy game of race cars in the middle of the bitumen. It was getting dark. A car coming along the road may not see him in time.

"Get off the road!" I yelled at the little boy while I tied the dogs' leads to the gate. "Come on, Jamie. You'll get run over."

"Brroomm! Brroomm!" he declared, completely ignoring me.

I scooped the little girl out of the puddle and hitched her up onto my hip. She smiled at me, dimples in both cheeks. Giggling, she rubbed mud over my face. "Kat eat," she said, pushing mud into my mouth.

"Not today thanks, Charlotte," I spluttered, which made her laugh harder. "Kat not hungry."

"'Morrow?"

"Yes, maybe I'll be hungry tomorrow and we can play a game of morning-tea then."

Even covered in mud the little girl was adorable. I hugged her to me and bent down to pick up Jamie's two cars from the middle of the road.

He let out a scream loud enough to be heard in faraway Timbuctoo. And then he punched me in the stomach. "Go 'way! They're *my* cars!"

"Ouch!" Not a bad punch for a four-year-old. Look out all the contestants in the current mosquito-weight boxing division. "Come on, big fellow," I said, holding my stomach with one hand and moving back toward the gate. "Let's set up a race course on the driveway. I have a real flag in the shed we can use to start the race off. And I also have some chocolate bars in my coat pocket. We can present a chocolate to the driver of the winning car."

"They're *my* cars!" he whined, but at least he followed me through the gate. I'd like to imagine it was my magnetic personality, but guess it was more likely the promise of chocolate.

I shut and locked the gate behind us, told the four dogs to wait, I'd be back in a jiffy, and headed for Mary's tent.

Pushing open the flap, I strode inside, baby Charlotte on my hip and Jamie brrm brmming his two cars as he ran from side to side behind me. Mary sat cross-legged on the dirt, meditating. She stared at nothing, mind somewhere in space. I placed Charlotte on the ground, tickled her on the tummy and then bent down to yell in her mother's ear. "Mary! Wake up! I found these two on the road waiting to be turned into roadkill."

Mary blinked. Stared at the children as though she couldn't quite work out who or what they were. And finally, her eyes began to refocus. "Um…sorry," she said and shook her head as if still attempting to dismantle the cobwebs and return to the real world. "They were supposed to be playing on the driveway."

"Well it seems your entrepreneur son has discovered how to unlock my front gate." I could feel myself getting a bit snippy. "You need to keep a closer eye on them. And look at Charlotte. It's freezing outside and she's in nothing but a nappy and a thin tee-shirt. Her legs and arms are blocks of ice."

A look I'd never seen before passed over Mary's face. Hate? Fear? Rage? Not just anger—but rage—pick up a gun and shoot someone, rage. If looks could kill, I'd be flat on my back with zero heartbeat. There was a moment's silence but when she did speak her words were slow, pointed, and simmering with threat. "Are you implying I'm not capable of looking after my own children?"

"No, no, of course I'm not. I'm saying, I found your children on the road. There could have been a bad accident."

"You know what?" she snarled, grabbing Charlotte off the ground and hugging her close. "It's people like you, no kids of your own, who are the worst. How can I be expected to watch them twenty-four-seven?" And then her face crumbled and she began to cry. Sheesh. Talk about sensitive.

"Hey, come on, Mary, the kids are fine, now. Look, first thing in the morning I'll change the latch on the gate so Jamie can't open it. Okay?" I sort of patted the woman on the head like I did with Lucky when she needed reassurance. "And I'm sorry if I upset you. Seeing the kids on the road scared me. Okay?"

The patting on the head clearly wasn't doing the trick, so I tickled Charlotte's tummy again, making her giggle, and left them to it.

Mary's volatile reaction to me after I accused her of neglecting her kids had me thinking. Tinkerbelle, the Earth Mother, was always complaining about Mary's lack of parental control. Always disparaging the manner in which she fed, dressed and disciplined her children.

It posed another question in this highly-complex mystery. If she was under threat of being reported to the authorities for neglecting her children, was a quiet, mystical woman like Mary, capable of murder?

12

Next item on the agenda. Cajole, pinch, or if necessary, beat information out of my sister, Liz.

Dragging my inner *Bombshell Chick* out of retirement, I presented Tater and Lucky with a doggy treat, switched the television on to Doctor Harry's Practice for their entertainment, and stomped up the stairs to my guest bedroom. Shoulders back. Jaw rigid. At the top of the stairs, I stopped and sniffed. Eeuwww! What was that disgusting, nose-curling smell? Scott must have dropped a pair of his socks somewhere on the landing. Socks and jocks. That seemed to be all the guy wore since Liz installed him in her bed. Odd really, as Liz wasn't normally into happy families. She was more into one night stands.

I shuddered at the thought of what this might mean. Scott and his socks and jocks as a future brother-in-law?

I knocked on the bedroom door. "Liz, it's Kat. We need to talk."

No answer. Only the escalating squeak of bed springs.

I banged again. Louder. "Liz, answer the door or I'll go downstairs, get the key, and open the door myself." The squeaking grew stronger, more insistent. "And if I have to do that, I'll bring a bucket of ice water with me to cool you two down."

Two minutes later the door opened an inch. The smell of dirty clothes, fast food and sex trickled out. My sister stood there in nothing more than a robe, which she hadn't bothered to do up. "You can't come in now, Kat. I'm busy."

"As if I'd *want* to go in." I screwed my nose up at her. "Scott, wearing socks and jocks day in day out is one thing, but Scott *without* his socks and jocks is another. No, I need information and only you can give it to me. So, little sister, tear yourself away from the hibernating tortoise occupying your bed, do up your robe like a good girl, and follow me downstairs. I have coffee brewing and you have questions to answer." A look of shocked surprise crossed Liz's face. "Yeah, the worm has turned, sweetheart."

After not being in my younger sister's life for the last five years, I'd been bending over backwards trying to make up for lost time. But I'd had enough. Hey, was no-one else worried about a manipulative killer wandering around loose? Or the fact that our mother was banged up in jail for a crime she didn't commit?

Without a word, Liz pulled her robe around her, did up the sash and stepped outside the room, closing the door behind her. She still hadn't spoken a word by the time we were both settled at the kitchen table, cups of coffee in front of us.

"I spoke to Babette's mother today," I said, frowning at the way Liz's bottom lip stuck out, exactly like it used to when she couldn't get her own way as a child. "And for goodness sake, cut out the little girl stuff. You're not six any more, Liz. We have a huge problem on our hands and I need your help to fix it."

"Why should I? Ma hasn't spoken to me for five years."

"And have you bothered to try to speak to her during that time?"

Liz's answer was a loud sniff.

"Liz, it's not just Ma we've got to worry about here. What about the real murderer? He or she is still out there. Doesn't that scare you? Even a little bit?"

"I've got Scott to protect me."

"Scott?" I almost choked on my spit. "How can he protect you? To have Scott's protection, you'd first need a forklift to get him off the bed and down the stairs."

"Scott took a lot of carbon monoxide into his lungs when those thugs tried to do away with him. It'll take time for him to get over it."

I thought back to the way Scott had looked when I found him unconscious in his car, the windows blocked, the engine running and a hose reaching from the exhaust pipe through a window into the car. It had been touch-and-go for a while whether he'd survive. If I'd been two minutes later, he wouldn't have made it. "I guess so," I said looking at Liz over the rim of my cup. "But he's certainly milking his illness for all he can get."

"I know." Liz grinned, lifted one eyebrow. "But I rather enjoy playing nursie with him."

"Ugh! Please! Spare me the details."

"And sometimes," she went on, ignoring me, "he plays the doctor." Her grin widened. "And when the doctor orders me to take off all my clothes so he can examine me, of course I obey. And why wouldn't I? What Doctor Scott does with his probing, exploratory fingers and tongue has me screaming for the big procedure, in less than a minute."

I closed my eyes and sang *lalala* in my head. I so did not want to hear the details of my little sister's sex life. Although, when Ben arrived home, I figured we might dress up and play doctors and nurses too. Just out of curiosity, of course, nothing to do with the probing, exploratory fingers and tongue. "Liz," I said, forcing myself to get my thoughts out of the bedroom. "I do *not* want to know what you and Bed-Boy get up to in my guest room. What I *do* need from you is the marital status of all the women camped out on my front lawn."

"Why?"

"I found out today that Babette, the woman who went missing during your demonstration, is in a relationship with one of their husbands. It might help the investigation to find out which one."

"That bitch!" Liz's lips pressed together in a grim line. "Not that I'm surprised, mind you. Babette has always flitted from one guy to the next."

I bit my tongue. No need to start World War Three by commenting on the fact that until Liz shacked up with Scott, that's exactly what *she* did.

Liz shook her head. "When we were living at a commune in Queensland, that woman caused a marriage to break up. And then, once the husband left his wife, Babette up and dumped the poor sap. Honestly, she's nothing but a man-stealer. Doesn't really want the guy, she's just obsessed with winning, or some such crap." Liz's frown deepened. "I even caught her trying it on with Scott, last week. So brazen too. The bimbo waltzes up the stairs into our room, while I'm not there, of course, and presents him with a big bag of grapes to make Scotty-Wotty feel better—*her* words, not mine. And then, the slut starts fluttering her eyelashes at him, wanting to feed him the grapes, even though he tried to tell her he was allergic to them. Huh. Tell you what, when I found out, I told her in a blast of four-letter words, if she didn't get her grubby paws away from my man and find one of her own, I'd deck her."

I kept my eye-roll to myself. Who in their right mind would want to steal a guy who spends twenty-three out of every twenty-four hours, every day, lying on a bed? "So," I broke in. This was all very interesting but discussing Scott's attributes was not helping my investigation. "Who's married and who's not?"

Liz gave a quick glance over her shoulder, decided no one could hear her other than Tater and Lucky who'd grown bored with Dr. Harry and come to sit one each side of my chair—probably in the hope of a dropped biscuit crumb. "Okay," she said. "Don't know if this will help, but here's the gist of my friends' marital status. Mary's bringing up her two kids on her own as both fathers have taken off to parts unknown, Mystique's single and proud of it, Spirit's married with an eight-month old baby—yeah, I know, who'd have guessed—Sienna's single, and Greta lives with her partner whenever she's not on the road working as a professional protester."

"And what about Tinkerbelle?"

"Tinkerbelle is…was…married." Liz paused, smoothed down one

side of her bed-hair and frowned. "Hell, I wonder if the police have notified Steve of her death."

"Steve? Her husband? What's he like?"

"An asshole, as far as I can gather. Funny thing though, Tinkerbelle was always into everyone else's business, drove us mad at times, but she was pretty tight-lipped about her own life." Liz took a sip of her coffee and placed the cup back on the table. "Heard her husband knocked her around a bit. Always had a ran-into-the-door kind of excuse when she rocked up with a black eye, but she never said a bad word against him. Loved the creep. God knows why. And jealous? She was insanely jealous of any female who glanced his way."

"And now Babette and Steve have hooked up…"

"…and Tinkerbelle's dead," Liz finished, her eyes growing as round as marbles.

"Think there's anything in it?" I asked. 'You know these people. Would Babette or Steve kill Tinkerbelle?"

"As I said, I don't really know Steve very well. As for Babette…she's man-hungry…but a murderer?" Liz shook her head. "No, that's going too far. And what motive would they have?"

I let out a deep breath. "Well, if Babette's in love with Steve and Tinkerbelle wouldn't give him up, the only way to get what she wanted would be to put the competition out of action. There's your motive for Babette."

"But she travelled to the city with us in the kombi van."

"And she could just as easily have travelled back home again in a taxi."

Liz pushed back from the table. "I need wine. Coffee's not doing it for me." She snaffled a bottle of wine from the bottom of my cupboard and wandered back to the table with the bottle and two glasses in her hands. "You joining me?"

I nodded, and then continued to outline my theory. "Babette could have asked the taxi-driver to drop her out the front, hidden inside one of the tents on the lawn until she saw Tinkerbelle on her own. And then she either fought with Tinkerbelle, knocked her over and killed her accidently—or—she snuck up behind Tinkerbelle and intentionally bashed her over the head, dragged her to the sand pit and buried her." I took the glass of wine Liz offered me. "There you go…Babette had motive, opportunity and means."

Liz emptied half her glass in one go, wiped her mouth with the back of her hand, and let out a sigh. All this was a bit too much like the *real* world for my New Age, hippy sister. "And what about Steve?" she said, eyes wide. "He's the violent one. We don't even know where he was at the time Tinkerbelle was murdered."

"Okay, you said Tinkerbelle was clingy. Let's say Steve wanted out of the marriage and Tinkerbelle wouldn't let him go. Or better still, maybe Steve had a life-insurance policy to be collected on his wife's death. What if Steve was in deep with the bookies, or a drug dealer, and needed money in a hurry?" I took a sip of my wine. Hey, this was fun. I was on a roll here. Give me a pen and note-book, or better still, a computer, and I could write a best-seller. I took another sip of wine, waved the glass at Liz, and went on. "Okay, what about this? Steve is sitting in his car nearby, watching and waiting for an opportunity to talk to his wife alone, sees Ma's out of the picture, and pounces. He pressures Tinkerbelle for money, she refuses, and so he belts her over the head until the insurance money is in the bag, and then buries her in the sand pile."

Liz stood up, grabbed the wine bottle by the neck and shook her head at me. "You're sick, Kat," she said. "You're turning all my friends into monsters. Anyone passing by could have killed Tinkerbelle." She grasped the neck of the wine bottle more tightly and headed for the stairs. "I'm going back to bed and I advise you to take a cleansing shower and then spend half an hour meditating. Your head is full of shit."

I watched her go. Maybe I'd gone overboard a little with my theories, but hey, Tinkerbelle was dead, Ma was in jail, falsely accused, and it looked like I was the only one in this dysfunctional mob, which included my sister and her more-than-weird friends, interested in proving Ma's innocence and finding the real killer.

13

"YES, BEN," I growled into my mobile phone. "I know I promised to ring you whenever I left the house, but that's an impractical promise. Only if I think it's necessary is a more realistic promise."

It was almost 10pm. I'd finished grilling Liz, shared a family-sized margarita pizza with Tater and Lucky, wasted an hour scrolling through Facebook catching up on what my cyber friends were up to and now I was dressed in black tights and my warmest and most unattractive nightdress. I figured Ben couldn't see how I looked, so why freeze my ass off in a baby-doll, almost-nothing-there nightie, when everyone knows thick ugly flannel is the way to keep warm on cold winter nights.

Ben let out a deep growl in answer to my more realistic promise. "Not happening, Kat. Why? Because your idea of *necessary* and mine rarely match up. How about, every time you get into your car you send me a short text before turning the key? That's all I'm asking. A short text."

"What? Like—I'm off to buy a packet of tampons?"

An even deeper growl came through the phone. "Or—I'm off to meet a killer."

"But Ben–"

"Come on, Kat. Just humor me, okay? It's scaring the bejesus out of me knowing you're in danger and I can't be there for you. Remember,

I know first-hand the trouble you can get yourself into." He gave a frustrated sigh and I imagined him closing his eyes and running one hand through his thick dark hair. "Why can't you be like a normal girlfriend?"

I frowned, felt a cold lump form in my chest. "Define normal girlfriend?"

"You know…*normal*. A girlfriend who makes me sweat every time she goes out with the girls and gets herself dead drunk. Not one who takes the risk of being *real* dead because she's chasing a psychotic killer."

I narrowed my eyes at the phone. "Hey, I can get drunk. I can even vomit all over you, if that's what you like." And then I felt sorry for the poor guy. After all, this was my Ben, the man I was hoping to spend the rest of my life with. I let the anger trickle away. "Okay, okay. I'll text you before I go anywhere. I promise. Just don't complain about the girlie secrets I'll be letting you into."

"Hey, babe. Talking about letting me into your girlie secrets," he crooned, his voice taking on a sexy timbre. "Tell me, in infinitesimal detail, what are you wearing?"

Uh! Oh! I pulled my granny-style flannel nightie, starring pictures of Pooh Bear and Piglet, more tightly around my legs and reached for my fluffy Panda hot water bottle. Then I set my voice a couple of octaves lower and used my imagination. "You know those fishnet stockings you love so much…"

"Ooh yeah…"

"I'm wearing them with a ruffled blue garter-belt and six-inch spiked high-heeled shoes. Prostitute red. You know, the fuck-me ones with the itty-bitty straps that wrap around my ankle…"

The gurgle Ben made sounded like he'd just swallowed his tongue.

"And I'm lying on my back, legs spread, nipples at attention, thinking of you…"

"Oh, babe, you sound good enough to eat."

Good enough to eat? Oh God. I could feel damp heat pooling down there where most of the best eating gets done.

"And what else are you wearing, babe?"

I swear I could hear Ben licking the phone.

"Nothing. Not a stitch more…"

"Ooh, I love it when you lie through your teeth, just to get me horny."

I laughed, sat up and wrapped my arms around my flannel-covered knees. "Okay, I've done my job. Now it's your turn. What are *you* wearing, Benny Boy? And I want to hear all the specifics, in 3D technicolor."

*****

It was ten o'clock the next morning. I'd slept like a baby—or a woman who'd had great phone sex—finished working the race-team, hydro-bathed the three dogs that'd raced at Gawler and now Liz and I were on our way to Wild Horse Plains. Our plan? To question Steve. Pressure him. Find out exactly how tight his alibi was for the time of his wife, Tinkerbelle's, death.

According to Detective Inspector Adams, the guy didn't appear particularly upset when told about Tinkerbelle's murder, but had an iron-clad alibi. Still, you never knew what a sneaky woman *not* wearing a policeman's badge could worm out of a man if she asked the right questions. And maybe buttered up to him a little.

I still favored the scenario of Steve eliminating his tree-hugging, clingy wife so he could move on to prettier and younger things.

The bitumen road heading toward Wild Horse Plains stretched ahead like a continuous gray ribbon edged by harsh bush in every color brown in the spectrum. Seemed never-ending. At least we were through the heavy traffic and were now cruising along Port Wakefield road. I glanced in the rear vision mirror and could see Lofty, the big and ugly, but fastest dog in my race-team, stretched out on the back seat of the car, on his back, legs roached in the air. For today, he wasn't a race dog—he was our guard dog. Or more to the point, we were hoping the size of the dog might deter a wife-basher from bashing a couple of nosy women who weren't his wife.

And of course Lofty was more-than-happy to indulge in a car ride.

Not so Liz. I had to guilt, wheedle, and threaten my little sister into acting as my backup. I even presented her with her own personal can of pepper spray, as an incentive. Unlike me, she *knew* Steve, so he might talk to her. Our story, when I knocked on Steve's door; Liz was Tinkerbelle's friend, and as we were in the area we decided to stop and offer Steve our sympathy. Well, I thought it made sense. Yet it wasn't until I'd threatened to vacuum her room, toss out anything I considered smelly, including Scott, that she'd given in and agreed to accompany me. What were her exact words again? 'Okay, I'll come with you…but don't expect me to be good company.'

So far, all she'd done was sleep.

Before leaving, as promised, I texted Ben, and received a cute selfie of his tanned man-boobs in return—plus ten kisses and a warning to be careful. I smiled at the image on my phone. Ben was so proud of his man-boobs. He didn't need to be a gym-freak and ride bikes to nowhere or bench press useless pieces of iron to keep fit. Instead, he trained a successful team of greyhounds, helped maintain his dad's property, and in his spare time, assisted his brother with a herd of prize-winning cows. In other words, the man's entire lifestyle was a natural gymnasium.

When we passed through the little town of Dublin, Liz woke up and stretched her arms in the air. She yawned. "Are we there yet?'

I grinned. "You haven't changed much, Lizzy. You sound just like that little kid who always sat in the back seat when we went out as a family. The little kid who every five miles would lean forward, touch her father on the shoulder, and bleat, 'Are we there yet, Daddy?'

She grinned as I bleated the words—exactly as she used to as a six-year-old—and then let out a long, drawn-out sigh. "God, I miss him."

"Me too."

"When Daddy died," she began, her voice low, "all that was left at home was toxic waste. It just ate at my insides. I know you tried to comfort me, to look after me, but Ma changed into someone we didn't know. It was like living with a stranger—not a mother. A stranger who sucked our lives dry with hostility and resentment." She shook her head at me. "Honestly, Kat, if I hadn't run away when I did, I could have ended up taking an overdose of tablets or in jail with a life sentence for murder."

"I get where you're coming from," I told her and reached out to squeeze her hand. This was the first time Liz had spoken about why she'd run away from home, at sixteen. "Hey, even now," I confessed, with a grin, "whenever Ma gives me *that* look—you know the one—and then puts me down in front of my friends, I get a strong urge to dunk her in a trough full of sheep dip."

Wild Horse Plains, consisting of not much more than a general store, a petrol station and a pub, came into view. I slowed the car down. "Here, take this," I said to Liz and handed her the paper with directions to Steve's property. "I know we turn off and go down this corrugated dirt road, but you'll have to direct me from here."

The corrugated road continued on for several miles and then changed into little more than a goat track. It wouldn't have surprised me if a family of kangaroos appeared from out of the bushes and hopped along beside the car. "Are you sure we've taken the right road?" I frowned at Liz. "This is the middle of nowhere."

"Yep. And according to this diagram, Steve lives in that tumbledown house way over there. The one surrounded by broken down cars and other garbage."

I drove closer and wrinkled my nose. "Seems like our friend, Steve, isn't into pushing a lawnmower, disposing of his rubbish or bending his back to do any weeding."

I drove through the open gateway and parked close to the front door. Figured if we needed to wave the white flag and retreat in a hurry, it was wiser to have the car within jumping-back-in distance. Loud music blared through an open window. So loud, it's a wonder the roof wasn't rattling and threatening to lift off and blow away. The house, red brick, was surrounded by cars of every color, shape and condition. Some with a For Sale sign on the windscreen, but mostly crashed heaps in need of major repairs. Evidently, while Tinkerbelle spent her days picketing for lost causes, Steve generated a living-of-sorts by buying for next-to-nothing, cars that had been in a major accident, cobbling them together again with sticky tape and string, and re-selling them as drivable.

In an attempt to block out the head-banging music which was making my teeth ache, I peered around the yard, couldn't see any loose dogs, only a couple of poor skinny bull-terrier crosses chained up beside a rusty water tank that had been converted into a kennel. The sour smell drifting from their direction spoke of long-term fear and neglect. "Okay, Lofty, my darling, would you like to water the weeds?"

Lofty wagged his tail, indicating he was more than happy to oblige. I opened the car door and grabbed the end of his lead as he leaped to the ground. Then, in a hurry to show me exactly how much he was looking forward to watering the weeds, he dragged me across to what was once someone's pride and joy, a royal blue Volvo. It now stood, axle deep in weeds, its front end caved in as though a feral giant had punched it in the nose.

Lofty cocked his leg on the front left tire and gazed up at the sky, an expression of sheer joy lighting up his face. Then, bladder empty at last, he eyed the crazily barking dogs attached to the converted tank-stand with interest. He gazed up at me with those mismatched eyes that got to me every time. 'Would you like me to go have a word with those mutts?' his expression seemed to ask, politely of course, but ready for action if I said the word.

I shook my head at him and joined Liz at the front door. "Try knocking harder," I told her. "His music's so loud he probably can't hear over it."

Liz moved from foot to foot, glanced longingly back at our car. "Steve isn't answering. He's obviously not home."

"Of course he's home. Who do you think turned that racket on?" I lifted one hand and thumped on the front door until my fist, bruised and sore, finally flew the white flag in resignation. "Steve!" I yelled in a voice loud enough to be heard in the next state. "Open the door!" And then, just in case he was wielding a baseball bat, I added, "Please?"

The door opened a crack and then a head poked out. A head covered in a shock of ginger hair that had likely seen a brush half a dozen times in the last month. "Yeah," he said, coming all the way out. "What do ya want?" He sniffed, his eyes on my Ford station-wagon. "You here to sell your heap of junk, or to buy one of my fully-serviced, reconditioned as-new autos?" He smirked, his bloodshot eyes undressing us both with a casual raking look. "Be nice to me and I might even throw in a couple extra tires."

Be nice to him? I wanted to put my finger down my throat and puke. "No, we're not after a car," I growled. "We came to see you."

"Me?" He stepped back inside the house, one hand on the door ready to slam it in our faces. "What do you want?"

Liz sent a quick frown in my direction, obviously telling me I was going about this the wrong way, before walking across to a white Mini-van that had obviously been in an accident in which it had rolled at some time in its near-past. The dents in the roof of the car had been belted back into semi-shape, leaving the entire vehicle on a slight tilt. "*You* mightn't need a car," she said to me, "but I'm on the lookout for one." She placed one hand on the hood of the Mini and looked up at Steve with one of her best flirty smiles. "How much you asking for this one, Steve?"

"How much you got, sweetcakes?"

Sweetcakes? Eeuuw! This guy had the charm of a crocodile.

Steve pushed through the front door, his salesman-face in place, and headed for Liz and the beat-up van. I swear I could see dollar-signs in his eyes.

"Depends," said Liz and moved to the back of the van out of reach of Steve's octopus-hands. "Does the car go?"

"Of course it goes," he growled, rolling his eyes. "Purrs like a kitten on steroids." Opening the driver's side door, he tugged a large ring of keys from the back pocket of his jeans, slipped one key off the ring and inserted it into the ignition. "Why not take the car for a drive, sweetcakes? Lots of power for a little car and hey, the color suits ya hair."

As the color of the car was white and Liz's hair was dark brown, I couldn't quite see the point of his last reference. Couldn't quite see what the heck my sister was up to either. Surely she didn't intend to go for a drive with this creep?

And leave me here on my own…

Aha! And maybe, while they were off test-driving the car, I'd have a sudden need to go to the toilet, in a hurry, like. And not being a male who can drag it out and spray the nearest bush in times of need, I'd have to go inside the house. And of course, while inside, I'd need to explore every room, you know, trying to *find* Steve's bathroom.

Maybe there was a future in the investigative business for my little sister, after all.

The moment the white Mini-van chugged out through the gate and tootled off along the goat track, with Liz at the wheel, hopefully keeping Steve from glancing over his shoulder, I popped Lofty back in the station-wagon, told him he'd been promoted to chief-lookout, and slipped inside the house.

Maybe I'd find Babette naked and handcuffed to the bedpost. Or curled up on the floor of the spare room, a thick chain fastened around her neck, the other end attached to a bolt in the wall.

Deafening music blasted through the house. I held my hands over my ears as I walked into the kitchen where Steve's sound system blared, the noise reverberating through my head like a dose of salts. Music? More like something from a nightmare involving a five-hundred-car-pile-up, interspersed with metallic thuds from a Medieval battle-ground.

Other than the sound system, only dirty dishes, greasy pots and fly-blown pizza boxes littered the kitchen. I journeyed on. Grease-stained overalls and dust bunnies large enough to start their own army ruled both bedrooms but there was no Babette staked out like a cross on either of the unmade beds. With only the lounge-room left to search, I snuck a quick peep through the open window. *Oh! Uh!* The little white van was chugging along the goat track towards home. I'd better hurry up and get the heck out of Steve's house before the wife-basher discovered he'd been conned.

This investigation had been a colossal waste of time. Babette certainly wasn't stashed in any of the rooms. In fact, there were no women's clothes or toiletries of any kind in the house. I shook my head, confused. How could that be? Both Tinkerbelle and Babette lived here at some stage. Where were their belongings? Unless Steve sent Babette packing after his wife's death and then burned anything left behind by either of them. But why would he do that? Australia was a free country. There was no law to say you can't have a wife *and* a girl-friend.

Unless Steve was covering up the fact that he'd murdered his wife.

I was almost out the door when Steve's phone rang. I stopped. Froze. Should I answer it? I glanced across at the fast-approaching mini-van. Was it worth the risk of being caught? Could just be his mother calling to remind him to bring his laundry when he came for Sunday dinner.

Or it could be an important clue.

Heart beating like bongo drums in the hands of a demented drunk, I dashed back inside the house and made a grab for the phone. All I could hear was a dial tone. Damn. But on a nearby coffee table, surrounded by empty beer bottles, a dog-eared *Hounded* dog-food brochure, and a blackened ashtray spilling over with soggy cigarette butts, a red light flashed on an answering machine.

Yesss!

One eye on the approaching white van, I pressed play, and listened, my feet already in the get-out-of-there-in-a-hurry stance. It was a man's voice. Well, it sounded more male than female. The voice was muffled, robotic, and steeped in menace.

'Be at the two wells, midnight tonight, with proof. I'll be waiting. No show—no reward. And no future.'

Proof? Proof of what? And what did the caller mean by *no future*? Sounded like Steve had fallen into a dangerously sticky web and he might have trouble extricating himself without losing his head to the resident spider.

On the other hand, it could be one of Steve's moronic mates playing a joke.

The white van shot through the gateway. I hurtled through the open door and scuttled over to let Lofty out of the station wagon. My philosophy has always been, 'you've gotta be safer with a dog', and although Lofty may be a pussy cat at heart—he was big. And big was always a plus when it came to protection.

"Well, how'd it go?" I asked Liz the moment she and Steve disembarked from the van.

"Umm…not *quite* what I'm looking for." Liz tried to close the car door behind her. Skew-whiff, the door refused to co-operate, so Liz left it open. The van was also missing a front fender now—probably dropped off somewhere along the goat track.

"Anything else I can interest you in?" Steve pointed to a bilious green-colored Holden sedan on the opposite side of the lot. The fact that the car had no wheels seemed to escape his notice.

"No, Steve, my sister doesn't want one of your suicide cars." I grabbed a quick breath and let my hand drop down onto the top of Lofty's head where I proceed to stroke behind his ears. Time to elicit some answers before Steve stormed off inside again. "Actually, we're here to talk to you about Tinkerbelle."

He scowled, his eyes narrowing into slits. "And what's my wife got to do with you?" He took a menacing step forward, either noticed the hairs rising along Lofty's back or the sudden mistrust in the dog's weirdly-colored eyes, and retreated. "I've said all I'm going to say to the cops when they were here, yesterday." He squinted at Liz, poked his chin forward on his chicken neck for a closer examination. "Hey, I didn't notice before, but don't I know you from somewhere?"

Liz gave him one of her sweetest smiles. She had a box full of them—

as well as an endless array of first-class scowls. "Yes, I'm Liz McKinley, a friend of your wife, and this is my sister, Kat. I spotted you a couple of times when you picked Tinks up from a rally." She switched from smiling, to a poor-you, big-eyed expression. I was so proud of my little sister's budding interrogation abilities. "Actually, we were passing by and thought we'd drop in to extend our sincerest condolences." She reached out to touch his arm, in comfort. "And ask what date you've arranged for the funeral service, so we can all attend."

"Funeral service?" Steve's frown deepened. "I've got no money to pay for the bitch's funeral. Her old man and the witch she calls her mother can do that."

What a lovely guy!

While he was discombobulated, I decided to jump in with another pertinent question. "Incidentally, Steve, where were *you* when Tinkerbelle was murdered?"

Steve's beady eyes fastened onto me like a rattlesnake, ready to strike. I swallowed a lump in my throat. Maybe I could have worded that question better. As Ben kept telling me, my interrogation skills needed a ton of work. "Er…just curious," I added and bit my bottom lip. My hand played with Lofty's large velvety ears, which felt soft and comforting. I could hear a slight rumble coming from the dog's throat. Also comforting.

"Not that it's any of your business, but I have a cast iron alibi." Steve snarled. Actually snarled, lips curled up off his teeth. "As I told the pigs when they came snooping around here yesterday, I was over the border in Victoria, delivering a car to a client."

"Well, what about Babette?" I went on, eying the way his fists opened and closed by his sides. This man had huge anger issues. "Your girlfriend went missing from the rally a couple of days ago and everyone is worried about her. Are you?"

He leaned forward and breathed stale tobacco and garlic fumes into my face. "Babette's a big girl. She can look after herself. *And* she's no girlfriend of mine. She's a bloody pain in the ass."

"Can we talk to her?"

"She's not here and I don't know where she is. Now, git off my property. And take your ugly mutt with you, before I set my two trained-to-kill, psycho dogs loose. They haven't been fed this morning, so they're sure to be hungry."

"Only this morning?" I came back at him as I opened the back door of my wagon and let Lofty jump inside. "Judging by the way the dogs' bones are sticking out through their skin, the poor creatures haven't been fed for a month." I smiled—or should I say, bared my teeth at him. "So, don't be surprised if an officer from the RSPCA arrives to check them out before the end of the day."

"What the fuck?"

"Goodbye Steve. Can't say it's been nice talking to you."

Liz flung open the passenger side door and took a dive into the car. "Let's go, Kat! We um…have an appointment at the doctors in half an hour."

"Hey, you! Dumb-shit!" Steve, eyes slits in his face which had turned a strange color of purple, strode toward my car. "If I see one sniff of Animal Welfare around here, you'll need more than a doctor—you'll need an undertaker."

"Seems like Steve doesn't want to answer any more of our questions," I said as I climbed into the car, locked the door, and turned the key in the ignition.

"You don't say," growled Liz, coming close to squashing the man's fingers in the top of the window as she battened down the hatches.

One eye on the rear vision mirror, as I took off in the direction of the gate, I could see Steve sprinting to keep up with the car. And heard his fists pounding against the back window.

"Don't forget, bitch! I know where you live!"

Sheesh! The gate post almost came to a sticky end as I accelerated out of his reach and veered off down the road.

14

Iᴛ ᴛᴏᴏᴋ ʟᴇss ᴛʜᴀɴ ꜰɪᴠᴇ ᴍɪɴᴜᴛᴇs for me to navigate the goat track and then bump our way along the dirt road into Wild Horses Plains, past the petrol station, and then out onto the main road.

"Which bitch do you think he was referring to?" Liz asked, her expression still a little anxious.

"Don't worry, little sister, *I'm* the bitch he's gunning for—not you." Although, to nut-jobs like Steve, every woman was a bitch. I shook my head in bewilderment. "What on earth did Tinkerbelle and Babette see in that guy? He's a Neanderthal. He should have been castrated at birth."

"Never too late."

I cut her a grin. "Hey, maybe that could be your anti friends' next mission in life."

"I'll put it to them…"

"By the way, you did well back there. Good move, giving me time to search inside the house."

She sat up straighter. "And did you find anything?"

"Well, there was no sign of Babette. No clothes, no personal toiletries, nothing. She either didn't go with Steve when she disappeared or he's kicked her out, lock, stock and barrel."

"So we got up Steve's nose for nothing?"

"Wouldn't say that." I lifted one eyebrow, grinned, and told her about the phone message. "And I know exactly which two wells our mystery caller is referring to. They're on the outskirts of the town named after the two historical water-wells that kept the early settlers alive back before plumbing was invented."

"So, what do we do?"

"We?" I loved the way my little sister had suddenly decided to join me in the investigation. Reminded me of how close we used to be as sisters. Before our Dad died. Before our mother turned into Satan's side-kick.

Liz stared straight ahead. "Tinkerbelle was my friend, Kat. Your reason for investigating her murder is to get Ma out of jail. Mine is because Tinkerbelle didn't deserve to die. Not like that, battered to death with a shovel and then left to rot under a pile of sand."

We drove along in silence while I steered the car along Port Wakefield road. Liz looked beat and I needed time to think. Who had the most to gain by killing Tinkerbelle? Steve evidently had a cast iron alibi, which I'm sure the police had already checked out. Babette still couldn't be found, although if she was responsible for bashing Tinkerbelle over the head, she could be lying low in another state by now. As for the rest of the women camped on my lawn—they'd been thirty miles away, at a rally in the city.

I was running out of suspects.

"What about Mary?" I turned to Liz, noticed she'd nodded off to sleep, again, and thumped her on the arm. "Where was Mary when Tinkerbelle was killed? I heard you tell DI Adams she wasn't at the rally because Charlotte had a temperature. So…where was she?"

Liz blinked and rubbed her arm. "Wish you wouldn't do that, Kat. I need my sleep. I didn't get much last night."

"Hey, not my fault if you spend the night bonking instead of sleeping," I told her without sympathy. "No wonder Scott's looking tired. He's supposed to be recuperating, not attempting to make the Guinness book of Records for the most bonks in a month." I shook my head at her, disapproving, but there was a trickle of envy creeping in there too. I was so missing Ben. Couldn't wait for the final of the Ballarat Cup to be run so we'd be back to bonking too. "If Mary wasn't at the rally—" I said, reluctantly shoving the thought of Ben, bed, and bonking to the back of my mind "—where was she when Tinkerbelle was murdered?"

Liz sighed, shrugged one shoulder. "Mary was at her mother's house. The baby was sick so Mary gave the rally a miss and took both kids to her mother's."

"Did the police confirm she was there?"

"Guess so, but knowing Mary's mother and her fondness for booze, she wouldn't know what time of day it was let alone where her daughter or grandchildren were at any specified time."

"Would Mary have any reason to kill Tinkerbelle?" I frowned, one eye on the side mirror where I could see a large black SUV looming up behind us. In fact, the SUV had pulled out from the petrol station at Wild Horse Plains as we passed and been four car-lengths behind us ever since.

Surely we didn't have a tail…

"Mary and Tinks aren't the good friends Mary would have you believe," Liz went on. "Like I said before, Mary was getting a bit lax with Jamie and Charlotte—you know, going off into a world of her own and neglecting them—so Tinkerbelle threatened to report her to Child Welfare."

"And did she?"

"Nah. Didn't have to. Mary loves her kids and would do anything not to lose them. She's been much more attentive since then."

But had Mary slipped back into her old ways? Had Tinkerbelle threatened to have the kids taken away from her, causing Mary to prevent that happening—at any cost? And then I remembered Jamie and Charlotte playing on the road while their mother sat in her tent meditating.

Still contemplating Mary as a murder-suspect, I checked my side mirror again. The black SUV was close behind us. In fact, it was too close. My mouth went dry. Was the car really following us? And if so, why?

I slowed down. The SUV slowed down. I gunned the engine and sped up. The SUV sped up.

"Hold on! We've got a tail!" I told Liz, gripping the wheel more firmly.

My sister peered into her side mirror and then turned around to stare out the back window. "Nah!" she said, settling back in her seat. "You're imagining things. Why would anyone want to tail us?"

Instead of answering, explaining how I seem to attract bad guys like honey attracts bees, I jammed my foot on the accelerator and veered off the main road onto a side road at the next crossing.

The black SUV followed me. Much, much too close. Like an angry black bear, sharp claws extended, gaining with every stride.

A sudden bone-jarring bump from behind rocked our car and swiveled it in the direction of the slippery grass-verge on the side of the road. Stifling a curse, I gripped the wheel harder, fought against the car's inclination to spear off the road and into a ditch. Liz let out a strangled scream. Lofty barked. I bit my lip, swallowing the metallic taste of blood as I wrestled with the steering wheel, fighting to keep the car on the road. If this was a nightmare, I wanted to wake up in one piece, not roadkill.

"Look out! Here he comes again!" Liz's cry ended in a scream as the torturous screech of metal on metal reverberated through the air. She made a wild grab for the door support, then tucked her head down between her legs.

I held my breath and wrapped my fingers around the wheel so tightly, the emergency crew would need a hammer and chisel to straighten them out again if they wanted to remove my body and take it to the morgue.

Just then, the black SUV, windows tinted, number-plate covered, flashed past my station-wagon, so close, it gouged a strip right along the side of the car, wiping out the passenger's side-mirror. The force almost took us off the road again. Then, warning, intimidation, or whatever their mission, accomplished, the driver left two inches of rubber on the bitumen and sped off with a screech of tires and a blare of the horn.

"Oh my God!" Liz gasped. "Stop the car. I'm going to be sick!"

I pulled up on the side of the road and sat behind the wheel, heart racing, breathing ragged. My whole body shook. From the top of my head right down to the tips of my toes. It was like I had no control over my body. The chill bit into my chest, into my stomach, my legs, my fingers. I couldn't move. I could hear Liz throwing up and vaguely, in a far-away land, hoped she'd managed to open the car door and lean out before she started hurling.

*****

"Did either of you recognize the driver of the vehicle?"

DI Adams, his tie stained with what looked like a blob of fried egg, sprawled on a chair at my kitchen table. Again. And like before, the moment he walked into my kitchen he zeroed in on boiling the kettle, collecting three cups from the cupboard and making coffee for himself and us. He even opened the fridge door and removed a carton of Long Life milk. All this, after settling Liz and me down at the table and fussing over us like a long-lost Uncle.

"Couldn't see inside," Liz told him. "The car had tinted windows." My sister's face was the color of dishwater and she looked ready to puke again at any moment. I leant across and squeezed her hand. Poor Liz. She'd tried to get into the act, tried to help me spy on Steve, but she really wasn't cut out for detective work. After all, her normal everyday hippy-life was slow, rural, peaceful. Far removed from becoming the target of some crazy person attempting to kill her. Thanks to the unwelcome snooping of her nosy older sister who'd dragged her out of a lifestyle of eating, sleeping, and bonking and thrown her head-first into the middle of a murder investigation.

After the tail end of the attacking vehicle had disappeared over the horizon, I'd examined Lofty and Liz for injury, rung the police and then

109

driven my poor limping car home. On high alert. Head swiveling. Eyes in the back of my head. Expecting a black SUV to come bursting out of every side street we passed. A black SUV with a crazed driver, intent on one thing only. To ram us into oblivion.

Luckily for us, 'the police' turned out to be the detective who was valiantly trying to give up smoking, DI Adams. Which meant we didn't have to explain the unexplainable to a stone-faced policeman who didn't understand the case. Or explain why we were embroiled in the investigation at all.

DI Adams reached across the table toward the koala-shaped biscuit barrel squatting in the middle of the table. He dug one hand inside the barrel, pulled out an Iced Vovo biscuit, and proceeded to dunk it in his coffee, leaving bits of coconut behind. "Could the driver of this vehicle have been Steve Brown?" he asked, between mouthfuls. "And remind me before I leave to give both of you a long lecture about the dangers of snooping into police business. This guy, Brown, is very volatile and easily upset. We've had our eye on him for a while now re flogging dodgy cars. By his over-reaction to your questioning, maybe *he* chased you and rammed your car."

"No, it wasn't Steve." I shook my head slowly. "This SUV was show-room quality, almost new, with tinted windows and lots of bling. There was nothing in Steve's yard like that. His specialty is selling wrecks. And anyway, we would have seen him following us when we left his house."

The Detective Inspector put his coffee cup down on the table, wiped his mouth on the cuff of one coat sleeve and let out a sigh. "Look," he said, his voice concerned. "There's something I have to tell you and I'm not sure whether your run-in with the SUV is related or not. It sounds to me like your mystery driver was sending you a message, a warning to stop asking questions and get the hell out of this murder investigation."

I sat up straighter. A warning? I'd been thinking along the same lines. But a warning for what? Was it somehow connected to the phone message on Steve's answering machine?

"I know you're trying to prove your mother's innocence, but you must stop asking questions, Katrina. It's become far too dangerous. Leave this to us. Next time they mightn't stop at ramming your car and driving off. Next time they could ram you over a cliff or nose-first into a tree."

They?

Next time?

My skin prickled and my stomach belly-flopped down to my toes. But what was the warning all about? And why me? I knew nothing. Not a who, nor a how, nor a what. So why had there even been a *this time*?

The detective's eyes left me and he appeared to brace himself as he focused on my sister, Liz. She looked up from the table where she'd been vacantly fiddling with a teaspoon. "I'm sorry to have to tell you this, Elizabeth, but we found your friend, Babette, this morning."

Sorry? Since when did finding a missing person, require an apology? A deep heaviness settled in my chest. Fear? Dread? I held my breath, glanced across at Liz, and waited for the knockout blow.

"Babette?" Liz rolled her eyes. "Whose husband was she in bed with this time?"

"I'm sorry to say we found your friend in the Port River. She'd been battered to death with a blunt instrument and thrown into the water. Her body washed up at Pelican Point this morning."

My heart stopped beating. Actually stopped beating for what felt like forever. I wasn't seeing the adult Babette washed up on the river bank. No, I was seeing a little girl in a tutu, a big smile on her face. An innocent little girl and a loving mother who feared this day would come.

"Noooo!" Liz, her face waxen, her eyes haunted, lurched from the chair and ran stiff-legged in the direction of the bathroom.

She didn't make it. I could hear her crying and throwing-up at the foot of the stairs.

15

I WAVED TO THE DETECTIVE AS HE pulled out of the gateway.

Another of my front-lawn campers murdered. A shiver skittered up my spine and I tugged the light rain coat I was wearing more firmly around my body and slid the zip right up to my chin. Who'd have thought a protester's life could be so hazardous? Liz should have stayed in the safety of that quiet hippie commune in Queensland, where the biggest drama of the year was a verbal altercation between her and whoever pinched one of the pumpkins she grew in her little patch of ground. Much safer than being involved with these weird new friends who were a mixture of New Age mystics and hard-nosed antis.

After I'd cleaned the vomit from the floor, wiped Liz's face with a damp flannel and listened to her ranting—she'd never help me with another investigation, this place was jinxed, I was the cause of her friends dying, she was going to pack up and get the hell out of my house and never come back—I left her to a surprisingly tender, Scott. He wrapped her in his arms and shook his head at me as if to say, don't worry, she's a bit highly strung, but that's okay, I love her.

Well that's what I interpreted his head-shake as saying. Could also have been, you're a moron for taking your sister to question a suspected killer and if she gets hurt, I'll know who to blame.

But I preferred the first translation.

Two of my racing dogs were booked in to see our local vet, Terry

Blackburn, at 1.30pm, so I couldn't hang around comforting Liz any longer. After the stress of the last two days it would be good to see a friendly face. Dr. Terry Blackburn was one big huggy-bear who always made me smile. In fact, he was due to be married the following month and if I didn't have the deliciously delightful Ben as my boyfriend, I'd be dueling with water-pistols at dawn with Terry's soon-to-be-wife.

The big guy was not only gentle and good looking, if it hadn't been for Terry, we wouldn't have known why thieves were after the two dogs I'd been fostering for GAP a couple of months ago. He'd discovered the microchips had been tampered with, which helped solve the Slow Dog scam that had the industry in tatters. Also, as the GAP's official vet, Terry gave his services to the program for the cost of medications only, claiming it was his contribution to the recycling of greyhounds from racing dogs to lounge-lizards.

As I entered the kennel house, I found Jake, sleeves rolled to his bony elbows and dreadlocks wet and shiny, washing dog towels and rugs in the big old industrial washer I'd had installed for this purpose. "Hey, Jake. What are you still doing here? You were due home for lunch half an hour ago. Go on, off you go. I'll put the rest of the rugs and towels in the drier before I take Suzy and Clark to the vet."

"Saw that detective guy here." Jake folded two blankets he'd removed from the drier ready to stack on the bottom shelf of a nearby cupboard. "Thought I'd, like, stick around and see if you needed me."

I smiled. Jake, for all his eccentricities would make some girl very happy one day. Of course, the girl would need to be as ditzy and laid-back as Jake or she'd emasculate him before their first anniversary. "I'm fine thanks, Jake. Can't say the same for poor Babette, though."

He froze in mid-fold. "Babette?"

"Yeah. You know, the tall shapely blonde with the pumped-up boobs. The one who went missing from the rally the day Tinkerbelle was murdered."

Jake nodded, gave a throat-clearing cough and I could tell by the red stain that spread from his neck to the roots of his hair that he *did* know the tall shapely blonde with the pumped-up boobs. Intimately.

I let out a sigh. "She's dead, Jake. Murdered. The police found her in the Port River this morning."

"Shit!"

I cast my eyes to Jake. He was a first-class weirdo, but Jake never swore. "What's wrong? Do you know something you're not telling me? Something that might help find the mongrel who beat poor Babette to death then threw her body in the river?" I took the folded blankets out of Jake's cold hands, put them on the shelf and got right into his space. "You do realize that whoever killed Babette most likely also killed Tinkerbelle?"

Jake blinked under my onslaught and staggered back. "Hey, dude, I know nothing about murder. I just thought like, Babs, she was a hot, hot mamma. Sizzling hot. The night before she disappeared she, like, spent the night at my pad. We made love." He blew out through his mouth, lips pursed. "And boy, did that hot mamma know all the moves. Next day I woke up, she was gone. Me? I was wiped out. Like, totally exhausted. I could barely lift myself off the mattress to come to work."

"Oh, I see."

"What if the cops, like, think it's me?"

"What do you mean?"

"What if the cops think I'm the murderer? Hey, dude, I was there, like, stalking Tinkerbelle, just before she was murdered, and I slept with Babette just before she disappeared." He covered his face with both hands and shook his head. "I'm toast, man."

I could see Jake's point. Cops often put two and two together and came up with twenty-two. "That's ridiculous," I told Jake who was falling apart in front of me. "No need to mention about sleeping with Babette. It's none of their business and has nothing to do with her ending up in the river. Like, days later. Now, go home, chill out and stop worrying. I'll finish up here and then I'm off to the vet. Okay?"

Jake nodded, his usually smiling face drawn. In fact, the poor guy looked ready to cry. Didn't know if it was hearing about Babette's death, or he still figured sleeping with her put him dead center in the frame. I threw an arm around his scrawny shoulders and squeezed. "Hey, Jake, you're a good guy. Now go home. Make yourself a cup of that disgusting herbal tea you love so much and stop stressing out. I'm on the case."

I shooed him from the kennel house and watched as, feet dragging instead of the usual dancing-steps, he hauled his bike upright, threw one leg over and pedaled off. A picture of misery.

So…I now had two good reasons to dig out and point a finger at this mysterious killer. Not only was Ma in jail, accused of a murder she didn't commit, but the police might very soon start harassing Jake.

*****

Dr. Terry Blackburn, his white vet coat splattered with what looked like brown medicine—or diarrhea—glanced up as I muscled his next two patients through the doorway of his vet surgery. Unlike most animals that visit the vet, my greyhounds were on the end of the lead. And if I hadn't grabbed the doorway with one hand and held on until my knuckles turned white, they'd have knocked their beloved local vet onto his very fit backside and proceeded to lick his face clean of any sweat or other foreign substance. All my dogs were more than happy to visit Terry Blackburn. They knew he wasn't just the scary guy who stuck needles into them or sliced and stitched them on the operating table. As well, there was always a welcoming treat, a cuddle, and an ear-scratch thrown into the mix.

"Hi there, gorgeous," he said and sent me his usual hundred-megawatt smile while digging into a large round jar and extracting several liver treats in an effort to ward off the excited dogs bouncing up and down at his feet.

"Gorgeous?" I raised one eyebrow in mock-horror. "I certainly hope you're talking to the dogs and not me, Sunshine. Now that your wedding date is *finally* set, after waiting—what was it, seven years—you can't call me gorgeous anymore. What would Becky, your ever-patient, fiancé think?"

He fluttered his eyelashes at me. They were long and thick and curled slightly at the ends. Always made me so jealous as mine are virtually non-existent. "Katrina, even when I'm an old married man with a tribe of angelic children, you'll still look gorgeous to me."

I grinned at his effusiveness. Couldn't help it. Terry Blackburn was one of those rare guys you couldn't take offense to. Now, if it had been Steve-the Sleaze, from Wild Horse Plains calling me gorgeous, I'd have spit in his face and backpedaled so fast I'd have been a blur on the horizon. Not so Dr. Terry. With his warm smile and irresistible dimples, he believed in making everyone he came in contact with feel good about themselves.

"Have you heard about this mysterious illness that's affecting some of our racing dogs?" he asked, his face now serious as he stripped off his stained vet coat and shucked his large frame into a clean one. "It's got us vets beat. Can't work out what's causing it."

"Yeah, scary stuff. I only found out at the track on Tuesday. Thought I'd better pull my dogs out of racing for a couple of weeks. See what happens."

Terry lifted Suzy, my little white and black bitch, onto the treatment table and inserted a needle into her track leg ready to drain the blood, thereby reducing the size of the lump. "Doesn't seem to be contagious," he said. "Not at this stage anyway, but it doesn't hurt to be careful."

"What's the symptoms?"

"It's quite bizarre. Seems to mainly affect dogs that have been racing well. Dogs that have a string of recent wins under their belt. First there's lethargy, then a freaking high temperature, and if you can't get the temp down within 24 hours, death usually follows."

"And there's no clue as to what's causing the illness? No drugs detected in the affected dog's system?"

"Nope. Nothing at all." He shook his head. "Okay, I have a theory, but I'm not voicing an opinion just yet until I've done more research. It makes me physically ill, seeing these poor dogs come in to the surgery and not knowing what to do to help them."

"And it's only greyhounds that are affected?"

"At this stage."

"Doesn't make sense."

He covered Suzy's track leg with a pretty purple vetrap bandage, lifted her down from the table and fed her another handful of liver treats. "You know what to do, Kat. Leave the bandage on for 24 hours to stop the swelling and then ice the leg every four hours for a couple of days. Should be fine after that." He rolled his shoulders. Ran a hand through his mop of in-need-of-a-cut hair. "Now, what's up with our boy, Clark?" He bent down to scratch behind the dog's ears. "Did those owners of his stuff him full of sweets and give him a bellyache?"

"They'd like to." I laughed as I tied Suzy to the table leg and then helped Terry lift Clark onto the treatment table. "Whenever he visits the RSL Aged-care Home, he walks around with a sign around his neck: I'M A RACING DOG. PLEASE DO NOT FEED ME. Of course, once he's finished racing it's out of my hands. Did you know, when he retires, he's going to live at the RSL full time as their Pet in Residence? He'll love that."

Terry's smile was tired and the bags under his eyes looked as though they were packed and ready to go to Hawaii for a long holiday. How much sleep the poor guy was getting while this unknown illness was killing greyhounds, was anyone's guess. Dr. Terry Blackburn was a dedicated and fanatic animal lover. Whenever he discovered a person being cruel to an animal, whether intentional or not, they copped it from him with both barrels blazing. "Let me know when Clark retires," he said, "and I'll personally visit the Home and give the residents a talk on what NOT to feed dogs and how bad it would be for Clark to become overweight."

"Thank you, they'll listen to you and abide by your rules. However, instead of feeding Clark the cake and chocolate biscuits they've been saving for him, they'll more than likely insist *you* eat the goodies."

"That's okay." He grinned. "I'm a big boy. I need feeding up."

I looked at his stomach. Although covered by his white vet coat, it was plain to see Terry had a sweet tooth. "You know, I might have to give *you* the talk about what you can and can't eat or you won't fit into that new suit you bought for your wedding next month."

Terry let out a loud guffaw. "And the future Mrs. Blackburn would *not* be impressed. Now, tell me, what's up with Clark?"

"He played up in the boxes on Tuesday, missed the jump, and didn't run on at all, which is completely out of character. I checked him out next day and found quite a bit of soreness in his right triceps, so I've been applying ice. Might need to inject it."

After needling Clark, Terry presented him with a handful of treats and helped me set the dog back onto the floor.

He looked at me, his mouth grim. I watched him lick his lips in thought.

"What is it?" I frowned at him. And then it clicked. "You want to run your theory on what's causing the mystery illness past me, don't you?"

"No, I don't."

"Yes, you do. You have that look on your face as though you're dying to bounce an idea off me. Come on, spit it out."

He turned away, sighed. "No, I'm not ready just yet, Kat. Maybe in a couple of days, when I've finished carrying out a few more tests." He turned back, screwed up his nose and let out another sigh. "Okay, I'll just say, don't feed anything new to your racing dogs until this is all over. Right?"

I nodded, still in the dark. "Riiight."

He winked at me, his grin creating a cute dimple in each cheek. "Good. I'm glad we've got that all sorted."

16

By the time I left the Vet surgery and drove from Two Wells to Virginia, a small township on the outskirts of a thriving market garden area, the earlier persistent rain had eased to a light drizzle. It was 12.55pm—almost Tanya's lunch break—so I drove slowly down the main street of the town and finally angled the station-wagon along the curb in front of *The Luv Bug,* the Adults-only store where my best friend earned her pay check each week.

Although my hair was rats-tail wet already, I pulled the hood of my jacket up over my head and, leaving the dogs in the car, made a run for it. Pushing through the frosted glass door of the shop, I could see Tanya and her on-again, off-again, once-again-smitten, policeman boyfriend, Constable Bob Simmons. They were standing together in the middle of the shop, molded from hip to forehead, *and* lip-locked. In fact, while waiting for them to pull apart from the tongues-way-down-throats' kiss, I counted to a hundred and fifty in my head. Slowly. Which sort of proves people don't necessarily need to breathe, to live. Bob was in his cop uniform and Tanya was dressed in a nurse's uniform. Not your normal starched knee-length conservative nurse's uniform. Oh no. This uniform barely covered the frilly pink panties she wore underneath, and the material saved by the size of the outfit could easily have been turned into a full-sized tablecloth.

While waiting for the two lovebirds to finish saying goodbye, sayonara, au revoir *and* arrivederci, I glanced across at the man behind the shop counter, and did a double take. It was Tanya's nerdy boss, Norm. Usually dressed in a conservative suit complete with lackluster boring tie, today his outfit consisted of long black boots, black satin breeches so tight nothing was left to the imagination, plus a batman's cape. His skinny chest, which reminded me of a chicken denuded of its feathers and ready for the pot, was bare.

"What's with the fancy dress?" I asked Norm as I sauntered up to the counter to examine a pile of fine-ribbed dildos that, according to the sign displayed above them, had come all the way from Paris, France. "You two starring in a porno-movie?"

Tanya waved and blew a final kiss to the departing Bob, then scowled across at her boss who'd ducked behind a large blow-up doll, pretending to check the price tag. "Ask Batman. He came up with this great idea that it might bring more business if we dressed up." Her scowl deepened. "Yet every time a customer slinks into the shop, the bare-chested guy-in-the-cape goes missing and leaves me to serve." She shook her head at him. "Not your most brilliant idea, was it, Norman?" She turned to me. "Come on, in the back room, Kat, and we'll have lunch. I've brought enough pumpkin soup and crusty rolls for both of us. Genius here can fly around the shop and check for bad guys, 'cos I'm done with playing Nurse Nightingale." She yanked the cheeky nurse's cap off her head, tossed it onto the counter and glared at Norm. "And after I've eaten my lunch, I'm getting changed back into my civvies. Right?"

Batman, whose nipples protruded like icicles on a frozen street lamp, nodded his agreement and reached for a shirt. "Okay, I admit, it wasn't one of my better ideas," he admitted through chattering teeth, "but you *did* manage to unload that expensive battery-operated raging-bull dildo. Thought I'd never get my money back for that one."

"Which means, you owe me one, Boy Wonder. *And* I'm not likely to forget it."

The back room of the shop was done out with a shiny-topped table and chairs, a stove, a two-slice toaster, micro-wave, an electric kettle, a desk with a state-of-the-art computer, and a couple of comfortable lie-back lounge chairs. Norm might be a nerd, but he was a comfort-loving nerd.

"Heard any more news about Tinkerbelle's murder?" Tanya stuck a large container of soup in the microwave and while it was heating, placed two bowls and soup spoons on the table.

While I told Tanya about what went on during our visit to Tinkerbelle's husband, Steve, I switched the toaster on and loaded it up with a couple of slices of light rye bread. There was a choice of butter or margarine in the refrigerator, so knowing we both thought margarine equivalent to rubber tires, I grabbed the carton of butter.

"And there was no sign of Babette having been there?"

"Nope. No women's clothes, no toiletries, nothing. Yet her mother seemed to think Babette was living with Steve."

"Maybe Steve killed her and dumped her belongings in the river along with her body."

"He's a nasty piece of work and I wouldn't dismiss him as the murderer," I said as I slathered butter on both slices of toast and cut them into threes, ready to dunk in the pumpkin soup, "but there seems to be someone threatening him too."

I told Tanya about the robotic message on Steve's answering machine. "Of course it could have been one of his mates sending him up, but even though the voice was disguised, you couldn't mask the menace behind the words."

Tanya slurped a spoonful of soup, ran her tongue over her lips and then raised one eyebrow at me. "So…we'll be hiding out at the rendezvous, listening to Steve and the Mystery Man's conversation at midnight tonight. Right?"

I coughed. The bite of toast I'd just taken, sticking in my throat. Actually, no, I hadn't thought about being in the same space as two potential murderers. Not in a heartbeat.

Tanya went on as though I'd nodded my head and given her the thumbs up sign. "The meeting is scheduled for midnight, so *we* arrive about 11.45, find a good hiding place and record every word they say. If it's incriminating, we take it to D.I. Adams and leave it to him. Simple. Now, what do you think of this pumpkin soup? I added quinoa and spinach leaves." Tanya took another spoonful of soup and licked her lips again. "Maybe a little too much quinoa. What do you think?"

Tanya could have added bird-droppings to the pumpkin soup and I wouldn't have noticed. My mind was still circling around the concept of being an uninvited guest at a midnight rendezvous involving two potential murderers. "But Tanya…" I bleated, amazed at the way she was cleaning up her bowl of soup as though she hadn't suggested we put our heads in the lion's den. "What if the message was a joke and no-one turns up?" Definitely the best scenario.

"So…we go home and warm up with a couple of glasses of wine." She stood up and carried her empty dish and plate across to the sink. "I know you're worried about your mother's incarceration and Jake confessing to sleeping with Babette the night before she disappeared, so this is an excellent opportunity to find out if Steve and the Mystery Man are involved. It's the first real clue we've had."

"I suppose…"

"I'm surprised you didn't inform DI Adams of the phone message."

"And what? Tell him I'd broken into Steve's house to search it? He'd have me thrown in the cell next to Ma. And anyway, what if the whole thing's a joke? If the Detective Inspector staked out the place with a dozen cops, only to find Steve's buddies waiting to douse Steve with water pistols and flour bombs, my life wouldn't be worth the cost of a used postage stamp."

Tanya shrugged. "Fair enough." She filled the sink with dishwashing liquid and hot water. "How about we leave from your house around 11.30? That way we'll reach the site about 11.45 and be well and truly hidden by midnight. I'll use my phone to record everything. That okay with you, Kat?"

Still struggling to force toast down my fear-induced, dry throat, I nodded. What else could I do? Tanya was offering to help me find the real killer which would mean Ma would be released and Jake would be back to being my happy-go-lucky, always smiling, dreadlocked assistant.

I tossed the remainder of the toast in the bin and took a sip of Tanya's quinoa and spinach enhanced pumpkin soup. Hopefully, by midnight tonight, I'd manage to persuade my quaking *Bombshell Chick* to come out of hiding, pull up her big-girl's pants, and help catch a killer.

*****

Four flat tires.

I stared at my crippled station-wagon in disbelief.

While I stood gaping, open-mouthed, at my car's airless tires, Tanya strode across to the front of the car and unhooked a piece of white paper from under the left windscreen wiper. "What's this?" She waved the paper in the air then passed it across to me.

STOP MEDDLING OR YOU'LL BE FLATTER THAN YOUR TIRES.

The words sent ice crashing in my chest like an avalanche. "Who did this?" I shook my head at Tanya and drew my coat more closely around my shivering body. "And how could they let down four tires, leave a threatening note and then walk away without anyone noticing? This place isn't exactly a cemetery. Jesus, it's more like Adelaide railway station at peak hour."

Tanya's eyes beneath her black knitted beanie looked huge, fearful, the moonlight reflecting a face paler than milk. "Shall I ring the police? Or do you want to talk to DI Adams himself?"

I shook my head at her. "What can the police do now? Whoever did this is long gone. No, I'll drop in and see DI Adams in the morning and give him the note. Let forensics or whoever take a look at it."

Tanya seemed rooted to the spot. She stared at the flat tires as though they were going to morph into poisonous snakes and bite her. She wrapped her arms around her body and hugged herself. "You

125

know," she said, clearing her throat, "if you want to give tonight a miss, Kat, I'll understand. We could always just go inside and open a bottle of that cheap wine you've got stashed in your bottom cupboard."

"Give it a miss?" I growled, straightening my shoulders. "Not flippin' likely. No time to pump up my tires or we'll be too late to catch Steve and Mystery Man, so we'll take your car." I waved the note in the air before screwing it into a ball and shoving it in my back pocket. "And as for this pathetic excuse of a warning? That just shows we've got them running scared."

Huh? That wasn't *me* talking, was it? No, that was my stupid *Bombshell Chick* persona poking her nose out of hiding. The real me, the one with a churning stomach, clogged-up throat and hands trembling so much I had to push them deep in my coat pocket to keep them still, *that* me—stood gaping like a fish out of water. *That* me was itching to object strongly, tell Bombshell Chick to get the hell back in her box so I could go inside the safety of the house and empty a bottle of wine with Tanya.

After all, the situation was getting serious around here and I didn't want to be as flat as my tires.

Flat meant squashed.

And squashed-flat meant airless, lifeless, cold stone dead.

17

*H*I BEN. CHECKING IN AS PROMISED. *Tanya and I are on our way to Two Wells to spy on Steve, Tinkerbelle's husband.*

When Ben's answering text shot back five seconds after I'd sent this message, I refused to check my phone. Okay, I'd promised to send a text every time I left the property, but I hadn't promised to read Ben's replies.

Due to the flat tire scenario, we were running late. By now it was 11.50pm and of course Ben would be expecting sexual innuendos and heavy breathing over the phone, not a text informing him that, although it was close to midnight, I was going out—not to Tanya's house, or to pick up a pizza—but to spy on a guy who was little more than a gangster. Maybe Tanya and I were being foolish, but I was even more determined to find the identity of the killer now that not only Ma but also Jake, my dreadlocked dude-helper, was a suspect. Hey, we only had the one clue and threatening note or not, this was too good an opportunity to miss. If we could reach the rendezvous in time to hide, Tanya had an app on her phone that could record the men's voices. Something concrete to take to DI Adams in the morning, along with the threatening note.

Tanya, after several swigs of something stronger than coffee from the hip flask she carried in her coat pocket—which meant I had to drive—was now over her shakes and raring to go. For the first time since she'd arrived, I really studied her outfit. And laughed. She was definitely dressed for the role. Black jeans, black raincoat, black boots and black beanie. I persuaded her to dump the black eye-patch, on the grounds she wouldn't be able to see where she was going and might fall into one of the historic wells.

My phone, buried deep in my black bag, began to play, *Can't Stop the Feeling*. I ignored it and after turning the key in the ignition, drove Tanya's Yaris quietly along the driveway and out through the gate. We were running late, but I didn't want to wake up the residents of Tent-City

My phone stopped momentarily, and then started up again.

Tanya looked at me.

I looked at Tanya.

"This is exactly why I didn't want Ben in the picture," I told her. "Keeping tabs on my every move is not a good way to maintain a healthy relationship."

"Well, I think it's cute." Tanya, rugged up in her three layers of black, hunkered down in the seat beside me. "Dan was always too interested in picking the winner of the next race at Morphetville to care where I was or what I was doing." She sniffed. "Which is why he's now my ex."

The insistent phone was driving me crazy. Ben wasn't going to stop ringing me until I answered. And if I answered—there'd be a big fight. So, I leant down and dragged my bag up off the floor and dropped it on Tanya's lap. "Do me a favor, Tan," I said. "Switch the phone off, will you? And when we get home, remind me to change the ringtone. If I hear Justin Timberlake singing *Can't Stop the Feeling* one more time, I'll toss my mobile out the window and then have to rake up the money to buy a new one."

Of course, driving to the site of the historic wells in Two Wells could end up being a big waste of time. But that message I heard on Steve's answering machine, if it was in any way related to Tinkerbelle and Babette's murder, was the only clue we had to follow. Plan A was to arrive at the meeting place early, hide in the bushes, and record the conversation between Steve and Message-guy. But now we were running late, Plan B was…

Well, we didn't actually have a Plan B yet.

From Lewiston, I drove onto Gawler road and headed toward the small township of Two Wells. No street lights on the main road and the sudden drenching rain made the night even darker. Maybe Steve and Message-guy wouldn't turn up. Too wet. I couldn't help thinking of my own lounge room with its warm gas log-fire and comfortable chairs. The picture of me cuddled up on the lounge, listening to television, Lucky and Tater snuggled up beside me, was very enticing.

No time for—

I almost ran into the horse. It was standing in the middle of the road. A palomino, with a white mane and tail that blew in the wind, and eyes that shone like beacons in the light from my car's headlights.

"Holy crap!" I yelled, foot stamped hard on the brake as we slid to a screaming halt no more than two feet away from the pale creature.

The horse didn't move. Just stood looking at us, water dripping from his forelock and running down his face. I swear he even grinned at us.

"It's Trigger," said Tanya, opening the passenger side door. "Aka Houdini. Damn horse is always escaping." She sighed and scrambled out of the car. "Guess we can't leave him in the middle of the road."

"No, but hurry up and put him back in his paddock or the meeting will be over."

"Hi Trigger. Not a good night to be playing hide and seek with cars on the road. You're safer on the other side of that fence." Tanya, black silk scarf blowing in her hand, bent against the stinging rain and walked up to the horse. "Come on, boy," she said, and while rubbing her hand up and down his nose, slipped the scarf around his neck and led him toward the open gate of the nearest property. She led him into the paddock, slid the scarf from his neck and gave him a pat on the rear. "Off you go, Houdini. And no more escaping tonight."

Tanya closed and latched the paddock gate and as an added precaution, used her silk scarf to tie the gate to the fence. Gate secure, she turned and splashed through the puddles back to the car. "It's two minutes to midnight," she said, peering at her watch and then shaking the worst of the rain from her coat. "We won't make it in time."

"Hey, with this foul weather, maybe we'll get lucky. Steve and Mystery Guy could be running late too." Without waiting for Tanya to finish buckling her seatbelt over her dripping raincoat, I burnt rubber and hit 80 from a standstill, before settling into 60mph as we neared the sleeping town of Two Wells.

As we passed the first building in the town, I switched off my headlights and slowed the car to a crawl. No sense in alerting Steve and his associate of our arrival.

It was only then, as I strained to see where we were going in the dark that I realized how vulnerable we were. The crushing gloom and loneliness of the surroundings seemed to wrap itself around us, offering no help. I should have let DI Adams know where we were going. These guys could slit our throats. Shoot us. Rape us. There was no-one to stop them. We were on our own Everyone in the small town was asleep and the noise of the rain and wind would muffle our screams.

Eeeeek!

Before I chickened out, did a U-turn and peeled off up the street away from possible blood, gore and personal pain, I parked the car under a peppercorn tree, 200 yards from the historic two wells site.

"Ready?" I whispered to Tanya as I slid my reluctant body from the safety of the car and peered along the street.

Nothing moved in the darkness, not even a stray dog.

"Guess so," whispered Tanya, melting into the blackness. "I'll have to turn my phone-torch on though. Can't see a damn thing."

"Okay, but keep it on low beam and when we get close, turn it off. We don't want to advertise our presence."

Fused together like Siamese twins, we slunk along the footpath until we hit the dirt track leading toward the commemorated two aboriginal wells, used by the first settlers in the area as a source of fresh water, and also giving the town its name.

"Quick, switch off the light," I whispered, dragging Tanya to the ground. "I can hear voices up ahead."

"But we're too far away to record," Tanya complained as we crawled through the oozing mud until we were hidden behind a thick bush. "I can't hear what they're saying."

"Better to be too far away than barge right into them."

"Yeah, but if we could crawl a little closer…"

Tanya was interrupted by a strident voice raised in anger. "Bullshit!" It sounded like Steve, and he was yelling loud enough to wake the dead. "You said I'd get paid half a mill for my silence, not a measly one hundred thou."

Beside me, I could see the Tanya bent over her phone and guessed she was busy recording Steve's words.

"I'm not some fucking weak-kneed bimbo like you've been dealing with in the past," he went on, and I could imagine the twisted snarl of rage on his face. "If I don't get paid half a mill, I'll take your Company's screw-up to the media. Television. Radio. And the press. Then let's see how you wriggle your way out of the shit you've caused."

"I wouldn't do that if I were you." The voice was male, so low I strained to hear it, but the menace was unmistakable.

"Just you watch me."

There was a short silence, broken by an audible gasp from Steve. "Hey, w-what are you doing, man?" His voice, which had gone up several decibels, came out as a dry croak. "No. No. Put that away. You've got it all wrong. I won't…"

The sound of a gunshot cracked the night air.

Holy catfish!

Heart beating like a set of wild bongo drums, I snatched up Tanya's phone and covered it with my coat to douse the light. Then, holding in a breathless whimper of fear, gestured to Tanya to get down. We lay flat on our stomach, face in the mud for what felt like half an hour but was probably only five minutes. We didn't move. Didn't breathe. Just lay there behind the bush, praying that whoever wielded the gun would hurry up and go wield it somewhere else.

I heard a car start and my prayer changed to please let whoever's behind the wheel drive off in the opposite direction to where we parked our car so he doesn't get suspicious and come check out the area.

We waited some more, until finally I was so stiff, I doubted my legs would hold me when I stood up. So cold, a hundred hot water bottles wouldn't warm me. And so scared, I wished I was Samantha from Bewitched so I could wiggle my nose and Tanya and I would be transported to my lounge room, in front of a fire and beside a table holding two glasses and an extra-large bottle of whisky.

From her prone position in the mud, Tanya rolled over and sat up. When she spoke it was like the volume had been turned down low. "Are we going to check and see if anyone's hurt?"

I wriggled closer on my stomach and then stretched my painful limbs until I was sitting upright beside her. My throat was so dry I needed two goes before I could get any words out. "Maybe we should just ring 000, tell them we heard the sound of a gun going off over near the aboriginal two wells and then get in the car and go home."

Tanya swallowed loudly. "Sounds good to me."

The acrid smell of gunshot tickled my nostrils. I wiped rain from my eyes, pulled in a deep breath and let out a sigh. It was no good pretending we didn't know what just happened. We had to go look for Steve. We had to find him and check to see if he needed help. My brain knew that—but my body had different ideas. Ideas that stemmed from self-preservation and the absolute abhorrence of seeing first-hand what a bullet fired from a gun could do to a person's body. I let out a sigh and stood up. "Up to you Tan, but what if the guy's bleeding to death somewhere over there? What if he needs immediate medical treatment?"

"Bummer." Tanya's caustic comment said it all.

By the feeble light of the torch we sloshed through the mud, heading to where we'd heard the raised voices.

"I really don't like this." I could see Tanya's head flicking from side to side as though expecting Steve to leap out at us at any moment. "What if he's only been shot in the arm or something and he sees us here?"

I stopped beside the first of the two old aboriginal wells and shone the torch down to the bottom.

Tanya convulsed in a full body shiver beside me. "If Steve sees us, he'll know we've been listening. And then he'll have to kill us to shut us up."

"No, he won't," I told her, my voice sounding like rusty razorblades scraping over bare skin. "Steve won't harm anyone ever again." Dizziness made my stomach roil as I stared down into the old well at the young man's crumpled body. His eyes stared back up at me, but I knew they couldn't see me.

"Is he dead?" Tanya whispered.

"Very."

There'd been so much rain over the last few days almost a foot of water lay in the bottom of the well. And Steve's head, marred by a hole in the middle of his left temple, was completely submerged.

18

AFTER CALLING 000, TANIA AND I decided against standing in the pitch black, in the pelting rain, babysitting the dead guy. We figured, if the body disappeared before the police arrived, it would mean the murder was a figment of our imagination—a much better scenario. So, we hightailed it back to Tanya's car where we stripped off our wet muddy raincoats, pitched them into the boot and sat, huddled together, motor running, heater turned on high.

Fifteen minutes later, Detective Inspector Adams, dressed in a long shapeless raincoat and a soggy felt hat, opened the back door of Tanya's little red Yaris and slotted himself inside. "Good morning, ladies," he said, his gravelly voice grating on the ears. "Nice of you to invite me out here at this ungodly hour."

I scowled over my shoulder at him. "Did you look in the well?"

"First thing I did," said the DI, his knees up under his chin. He shook his head. "Not a pretty sight."

I didn't push my seat forward to give him more leg room, just plastered my hands, palm out, in front of the small heater vents, in the hopes of catching every stray puff of warmth.

"Like to tell me what happened?"

For some reason I didn't feel like co-operating. Guess I was looking for someone to blame for the way I was feeling and decided to take out my perversion on the detective.

Tanya cleared her throat and half turned her head toward him. "Someone shot Steve."

"So I noticed. Any idea who did the shooting?"

"The guy who didn't want to give Steve half a million dollars," she said.

"Want to start from the beginning and tell me everything?" The DI sounded a touch tetchy. "Like, what the hell you two are doing at the scene of a crime? Why you decided to specifically visit the two wells site in the middle of the night? And how you just happened to stumble on a murder in progress but didn't get shot yourselves?"

I sighed and rubbed my nose, transferring mud from fingers to face in the process. By the sound of the barely-contained anger in the detective's voice, I figured it was time to co-operate. Being thrown in a cell with Ma would not improve my night. I sniffed, rubbed my sleeve across my nose and joined in the conversation. "Just lucky, I guess."

"Yeah, lucky the killer didn't see you, or you'd both be stuffed down the well in similar condition to the dead guy." He removed his soggy hat and shook his equally soggy head at us in bewilderment. "So…tell me, what are you doing at a murder scene, alone, and acting like a couple of immature and supremely stupid Nancy Drews?"

I refused to answer that one on the grounds it would only make me seem even more stupid.

Beside me, Tanya ran shaky fingers through her wet, bedraggled rat's-tail hair. She looked like she'd been squirted with a fire-hose then towed behind a moving car through a churned-up muddy paddock…which meant I was no beauty Queen either.

"Okay," I said, shifting my rear end into a more comfortable position on the damp car seat. "But I want your assurance that as soon as I've finished telling you our story, you'll let us go home. We're cold, wet and shivering, and it will be on your head if we catch pneumonia and die."

"Riiight!" The detective shook his head with that I-can't-believe-she-said-that expression he regularly got on his face when talking to me.

"Now, can you please get on with it? I'm not what you'd call comfortable sitting in this match-box of a car with my knees digging into my chin and *my* night hasn't even started yet."

"Well, I guess it's not what you might call the most sensible thing we've ever done," I admitted, while glaring at the enthusiastic head nod from my listener, "but here's what happened."

I told him about the message I'd heard on Steve's answering machine, my car's four flat tires, the threatening note under the windscreen and what we'd heard while lying on our faces in the mud, seconds before Steve was murdered.

Tanya plucked her mobile phone from the back pocket of her jeans and switched it on. "Unfortunately, because of Kat's flat tires and a loose horse called Trigger, we didn't arrive at the scene early enough to hide and record the whole conversation, but I did manage to document what was said just before the gun went off."

DI Adams, elbows resting on the back of the front seat, leant forward. "Excellent. Let's hear it."

It was more chilling listening to the recording of Steve's angry ranting and the icy menace of the other man's voice than when it actually happened. Now we were listening to the voices of a dead man and a stone-cold killer. Now we knew how it all ended. And when the gun went off, I jumped, bit my bottom lip.

No-one spoke for a long minute. Instead, I inhaled a deep breath, counted to five, held it for two and then let the breath out slowly. I could see Tanya's fingers nervously fiddling with her phone in her lap.

Time to go home.

I jammed the gear stick in drive and turned my head to stare at the man in the daggy raincoat and wet soggy felt hat. "So…can we go now, detective? Please. Or would you rather I screamed so loudly all those townsfolk gawking on the other side of the crime scene tape will think you're beating a confession out of us."

The long look he gave me indicated beating a confession out of me was rather tempting. Finally, he opened the car door and stomped one foot out onto the roadway. "Okay, you can go, but I'll organize for a couple of patrol-men to guard your properties until we catch this guy. There's a murderer out there and he'll very soon know you two were witnesses to his latest crime."

"Oh goody, thanks for reminding us of that, Detective," I said. "We'll sleep so much better knowing we're on an angry murderer's hit list."

"Go, before I change my mind." He slammed the car door behind him and then knocked on the front window to indicate he wasn't finished talking and wanted me to wind my window down. Then, he leaned in, his cigarette breath mingling with the acrid smell of damp car. "And," he said drawing the word out, "I'll see you both at the police station at 10am, on the dot, ready to make and sign your official statements. Right?"

"But I'll be at work," said Tanya.

"No, you won't," said DI Adams. "You'll be at the Elizabeth Police Station."

"Aye! Aye! Sir!" I touched my forehead in a salute.

One eyebrow doing push-ups, his lips quirked into a satisfied grin. "And now that your mother is not a suspect, I'll have her released, processed, and waiting for you to take home."

Nooooo!

And with that the curmudgeonly detective wandered off toward the hard-working forensic team, the hem of his long black coat dragging in the mud.

*****

Tanya's car barreled to a stop outside the Elizabeth police station. I stopped pacing the footpath and checked my watch. A minute to ten. Just in time. Dressed in her Love Bug uniform, she spilled out of the car and bolted across the road.

"Cutting it fine," I admonished, joining her as we pushed through the front door of the station and made our way to the front desk.

"Sorry, sorry. Norm had a meeting with a new rep who sells electric floggers and I couldn't get away."

"Electric floggers?" I rolled my eyes. "No, on second thoughts, I really don't want to know."

My nemesis, Constable Chalmers, aka Vinegar Face, who I'd had several run-ins with in the past, stood behind the front desk. Her face went into its usual lemon-sucking mode as we approached.

"Good morning, Constable," I said, all polite and sunflower bright. "I believe DI Adams is expecting us."

"I'm sorry, DI Adams can't be disturbed. You'll have to sit over there and wait." Eyes narrowed to show exactly how sorry she really was, Constable Chalmers pointed to a hard wooden bench running along one wall.

"So much for 10am, on the dot," mumbled Tanya as we tested the inflexibility of the bench by gently adjusting our rear ends to the concrete-hard timber. "Norm will have a litter of kittens if I'm not back by eleven. There's a busload of aged pensioners arriving from that New Age nursing-home that opened at Angle Vale last month."

"New Age nursing-home?"

"Yeah. They advertise free love, erotic movies, spin-the-bottle, you name it. One of the nurses who work there came into the shop last week to buy some ribbed dildos for some of the more experimental residents. She reckons they hold an Anything-Goes party there every Saturday night. And of course, physios and chiropractors and doctors are always on hand to treat any over-excited residents.

"You're pulling my leg?" My mouth opened in a disbelieving gape. I snapped it shut, but before I could urge my best friend for more juicy details, DI Adams strode into the room. He frowned at the constable at the desk who dropped her head on her chest and pretended she was busy filling in data on her computer.

"Ah, so, you're already here," he said to us, his face contorted into a closed-lipped grimace, which was his interpretation of a smile. "And here was me thinking I'd have to send a paddy wagon out to pick you up. Constable Chalmers should have sent you straight in." He stretched out one arm. "Just come through here and we'll take your statements.

It won't take long."

Yeah. Won't take long…

Three quarters of an hour later, I pushed through the doors of the police station and dragged in a deep breath of fresh winter air mixed with a lungful of car smoke as an ancient Holden sedan complete with mum, dad, and four kids stuttered its way past. Way in front of me, Tanya was yelling on her mobile to an evidently hysterical Norm, while running toward her car and waving goodbye to us with one hand. And beside me, Ma, dressed in the same wrinkled clothes she'd worn when I'd picked her up from the airport, looked a little dented.

Without a word she opened the car door and settled herself inside.

"Do you want to stop anywhere on the way home?" I asked her, checking the side mirror for traffic before pulling out onto the road. "A coffee? Chocolate bars? Potato chips? Big Mac?"

"I'm fine."

"No, you're not!" I snapped as I yanked the steering wheel to the right, to pass a van that had stopped dead in front of us. "And you're not making it any easier by acting like a prima donna. Getting through to you is such heavy-going—and it shouldn't be. You're my mother."

I blinked. Where the heck had that outburst come from? I snuck a quick glance across at Ma who sat ramrod straight in the passenger seat beside me.

"I need to talk to you and Elizabeth," she said in a voice so soft I had to strain to hear her over the sounds of the traffic as I maneuvered the large roundabout in the center of the road and drove up and over the railway bridge. "There's something important I need to tell you both. And after that, can you please take me home? To my house."

"What about the house-renovations?"

"I'll put them on hold for a couple of months."

"There's no need to go home, Ma. You're always welcome to stay with me." I cut her a quick glance. "You *do* know that, don't you?"

Ma reached across the console and patted me on the arm. I frowned, flicked another glance in her direction. Was that a thank you? An appreciative caress? A show of compassion?

Was the world coming to an end?

We traveled along Womma Road in silence, and it wasn't until we reached the corner of Womma and Heaslip Roads that I decided to move the conversation along. "Look, I know you've been through a tough time since you arrived back from overseas, and I'm sorry. What with the bad drug trip and then being accused of murder and spending three days in jail? It must have been a nightmare for you. But can you tell me who actually gave you the drugs? Surely it wasn't Tinkerbelle. You and she looked like ripping each other's head off when I left to go to the track."

Ma let out a snort. "Actually, Tinks and I ended up sitting down at the kitchen table drinking cups of herbal tea and eating cookies."

"Tinks?" I queried. "You were into nicknames at the finish?"

"Oh, yes. It was after that funny-looking guy with all the facial rings peeped through the window at us for about the fourth time. Tinks up and threw a heavy frypan at him—just missed his head by a whisper— and I threw a rolling pin. Then we both laughed at the way he ran away like a girl and mutually decided it was time for afternoon tea." She shook her head. "Guess the witch slipped something into my tea when my back was turned. And as for the cookies—I'm figuring they had more marihuana in the recipe than flour." She shrugged one shoulder and stared out the window. "Anyway, I don't remember much after that. It's all a hazy crazy blur. Woke up next morning stretched out on a mattress made of rocks and discovered a row of iron bars between me and the free world."

"So why didn't you explain this to the police when they questioned you?"

"Why should I? I was incensed. That moron, Adam, arrested me on such flimsy evidence it would never have stood up in court."

"Ma," I said, exasperated. "You could have been out of jail the same day if you'd co-operated. Winding DI Adams up wasn't doing you any favors. The man was tearing his hair out in frustration."

She laughed. A sound I hadn't heard from her for a long time. "Yes, he did get a bit agitated, didn't he?"

"Agitated? More like ready to ditch you in the toilet and pull the chain."

I looked across at the woman sitting beside me. This was more like the woman I knew before Dad died. A woman I could always talk to when I was a kid.

"What happened, Ma?" I asked her, determined to have it out. To get some answers. "When Dad died, Liz and I lost *both* our parents, not just one. You didn't want to know us. We couldn't talk to you. We had no comfort from you. We'd just lost our father and instead of having you to share our grief, you pulled away from us and turned into Godzilla."

"Let's wait for Liz, shall we? I had plenty of time for thinking while locked up in that bloody awful cell, and realized I couldn't go on living a lie any longer. That it was time to tell you both the truth." And with that she gummed her lips together and stared straight ahead.

I felt my breath catch in my throat and gripped the wheel tighter in an effort to keep the car on the road. "What truth? What lie?"

I may as well have been talking to the windscreen. With a small shake of her head, Ma continued to check out the herd of sheep grazing mindlessly in the paddock as we passed.

Thoughts in turmoil, I forced myself to concentrate on the road. What the heck was my mother talking about? I wanted to keep asking her questions, but deep down in that dark, scary, cobwebby place that sometimes shows itself in nightmares, I was afraid of the answers.

19

The moment I glanced across at the GAP dogs' kennels just inside the front gate, I knew something was terribly wrong. Ralph was jumping up at the wire, tail wagging, as usual, but Yolo, the little black bitch, lay in the dirt, unmoving, beside him. Even when I stopped the car, she didn't attempt to get to her feet. Just lifted her head and whined.

"Quick, Ma," I said, spilling out of the car and turning my head as I hurried over to the kennel-yard gate. "Help me lift Yolo into the car. I have to take her to the vet."

"But—"

"Now!"

There was no need to take Yolo's temperature. I could tell it had skyrocketed since earlier in the day when, as I'd been doing every morning since learning of the illness decimating racing dogs, I'd taken every dog's temperature, as a precaution. Yolo was hot to the touch, lethargic, and limp in my arms as Ma and I carried her across to the station-wagon and lay her on a mattress.

"You go inside and wait, Ma. Make yourself a cup of coffee and help yourself to whatever's in the cupboard. I have to go. It's urgent that Yolo gets immediate veterinary treatment. If our local vet can't get her temperature down, she'll die."

"I'm coming too." Ma, brushing black hairs from the front of her white cardigan, slid into the seat beside me and proceeded to buckle up.

I stared at her. "But-but you don't like dogs. They're dirty and smelly." Who was this woman I'd picked up from the police station? Had DI Adams made a mistake and released the wrong Mrs. Helen McKinley?

"For goodness sake, Katrina, would you stop babbling and just drive this poor dog to the vets."

A warmth, a sense of profound love spread across my chest, increasing to almost bursting point. I grinned at her, reversed the car and then jammed my foot hard on the accelerator.

We had a dog to save.

The moment I pulled the station-wagon into the car-park, Ma was out of the car and beetling toward the front door of the Veterinary Surgery. "I'll inform them we have an emergency and then come back and help you carry Yolo inside."

"Good idea."

By the time I opened the back door of the wagon, Terry Blackburn had crashed through the doors of the surgery and was striding out into the car-park, his kindly face creased in concern. "Temperature gone up?"

"Skyrocketed."

He frowned. "Kat, remember I said I had a suspicion about what was causing this illness?"

I nodded. Throat too clogged to talk.

"As a matter of interest, which kibble are you feeding your greyhounds?"

"Canine Plus. Always have."

"And you feed that to the GAP dogs too?"

I put a hand to my face and wiped my eyes. Why were we discussing kibble? Why wasn't he rushing Yolo into the surgery? "Yeah, I was, but last week I won a bag of that new super-duper new greyhound-formulation they're advertising on television, um…*Hounded*. Don't like changing the racing dogs' diets, so I decided to feed it to the GAP dogs instead. Why?"

"I'll let you know when I've worked out the final piece of the puzzle. Meanwhile leave Yolo with me. I'll carry her into the surgery and get straight to work on her. You go see Val at reception and sign any forms needed…and then go home."

"But—"

"Nothing you can do here, Kat. Please. Leave it to me. I'll get her temperature down. Trust me." He put an arm around my shoulders and hugged me to him. I wanted to cry into his white vet coat, but knew if I started, I'd never stop.

Instead, I stepped back out of his comforting arms so he could carry Yolo into his surgery, where I knew he would do everything in his power to bring that lethal temperature down.

What was causing greyhounds to get sick? Was it a virus? An infection? Had I inadvertently done something to contribute to Yolo's illness? What was Terry's interest in kibble all about? I wiped my wet face with my hand and watched the vet's broad back get swallowed up when the front door of the surgery closed behind him. I felt so helpless. Confused.

But all I could do was pray.

*****

I tucked my legs underneath me on the sofa and wriggled into a more comfortable position. On the other side of the room, my sister, Liz, sat ramrod straight on the edge of an armchair, a petulant expression on her face.

Our eyes were fastened on Ma, pacing up and down, almost wearing a track in the carpet. "I have something to tell you," she said, "that I should have told you a long time ago, but your father didn't want you to know."

"Oh my God," Liz sneered, rolling her eyes in derision. "Daddy was King of Zambania, a small island country in the South Seas, and as his successors, Kat and I are to be made joint-Queens and inherit buckets full of gold and jewels."

"Liz," I hissed glaring across the room at her, "stop being ridiculous

145

and let Ma say her piece. And Ma, can you please sit down and talk? You're giving us both a neck-ache watching you walk up and down."

Ma parked herself on the vacant lounge chair and clasped her hands together on her lap. She took a deep breath. "First of all, I want to say I'm sorry for distancing myself from both of you, especially you, Liz, after your father died."

"If that's all you've got to say after five years of not being my mother, I'll take myself back upstairs. Scott and I have some packing to do. We've decided to break away from the others and go look for some fruit-picking work up in Queensland."

"You always were the impatient one," said Ma, shaking her head at her younger daughter. "But what if I told you I wasn't your biological mother?"

Liz, half way through standing up, collapsed down on the armchair again. Her eyes wide, her mouth in fly-catching mode. "N-not my mother?"

Ma looked across at me and shook her head. "Nor yours."

I blinked. That bad trip on marijuana must have cracked Ma's brains and scrambled them like eggs. "What are you talking about? Of course you're my mother. I should know. I've known you ever since I was born."

"I could never have children," she went on ignoring my words. "Due to a bad infection not long after your father and I were married, I had to have a hysterectomy and my womb removed." Ma shrugged, seemed to study the pattern on the carpet. "Worst day of my life."

Liz, eyes chips of flint, leaned forward in her chair. "Well, if *you're* not our mother, who the hell is?"

"You see, your father always wanted to be a dad." It looked like Ma was going to tell her story her way. "So, we paid my sister, Sharon, to have you, Kat. Sharon was single, happy to give birth through IVF but wasn't interested in raising a child of her own. She was always in debt to the bookies and the poker machines, so was happy to take the ten thousand we offered her in exchange for a baby. And that baby was you."

"Aunty Sharon? My mother?" This was like being punched in the kidneys with the blunt end of an axe. I barely remembered Ma's younger sister because she died when I was about seven. But what I did remember, she was nice in an always-giving-me-presents sort of way, but she was a real ditz. Took me to the zoo when I was five and lost me the moment we passed through the gates. More interested in relaxing on a bench and listening the races on her radio than taking me to see the animals. So, I took myself. Found her still sitting on the seat an hour later when I got hungry and wanted something to eat.

"So…" Liz's voice had an edge to it. As if she was having trouble keeping it civil. "And whose kid am I? Was it the homeless woman you found wrapped in newspaper, sprawled on a park bench?"

Ma turned to Liz, her frown deepening. "This isn't easy for me, Elizabeth."

"Huh. And you think it's easy for us? Finding out the jaw-breaker we had for a mother all these years wasn't even our real mother."

Ma got to her feet so quickly the cushion she'd been leaning on, tumbled to the floor. When she spoke, the words came out as brittle as month-old bread. "Do you want to know or not, Elizabeth? If not, I will ring my neighbor and ask him to come pick me up right now. I'm tired, I need a very hot shower to wash the stink of prison off my skin and I want to get out of these clothes and then burn them."

Liz appeared to be holding herself together by a thread. And then, with a loud sniff, she crumbled. "I'm sorry, Mama. I just wanted you to hug me after Daddy died. That's all. Just to give me a hug and tell me you were there for me. But you didn't. Now I know why. I'm someone else's kid and you don't love me."

Brushing tears from her cheeks, Ma stumbled across the room and took Liz in her arms. "That's not true, Elizabeth. I love you both as much, if not more, than if I had gone through the pain of childbirth myself." She beckoned me over and enveloped us in a three-way hug. "I've been selfish and precious and instead of taking care of my two girls when your dad stupidly stepped in front of a truck, I got on my high horse and hid behind bluster and damaged ego and ended up running away from responsibility." She stepped back, took Liz's hand in hers. "Aunt Sharon is your mother too, Liz, but this time I had no knowledge of the consummation until my sister fell pregnant to your father. He'd fallen in love with her and planned to leave me once the baby was born. They were going to set up house together in another state."

Liz and I exchanged horrified glances. How could our wonderful dad, who we adored, do such a thing?

Ma sank back against the pillows on the armchair, her shoulders slumped, as though reliving this nightmare part of her life was taking its toll. "Sharon died giving birth to you, Liz," she said, her voice barely more than a whisper. "I brought you home from the hospital, a skinny little dag of a baby with a full-on attitude, and your father and I went on as if nothing had happened."

Liz shook her head. "You kept me? Even after Daddy and your sister betrayed you?"

"Of course. How could I not? You were the funniest looking baby I'd ever seen." She sniffed, then grinned, leant forward in the chair and lightly punched Liz on the arm. "No-one else would have claimed you."

20

Poor Ma. Fifteen minutes ago, when she waved goodbye through the open window of her neighbor's car, she looked ten years older than her fifty-three years. Sort of haggard, in a bone-weary, totally exhausted sense. I guess being accused of murder, sharing a jail cell with a couple of unwashed criminals for three days, and informing your two daughters you were not their biological mother, was enough to take the wind out of the strongest person's sails.

After Ma left, Scott—dressed in a sweater and jeans, as well as socks and jocks—took Liz off in the Kombi van. Liz said she needed to get away for a while, to get her head straight, so they were going to drive to the beach first and then to see a guy about some fruit-picking work they were interested in. Maybe there was hope for a lasting relationship between my baby sister and her dysfunctional boyfriend, after all.

As I headed down the driveway toward my GAP kennels to take Ralph's temperature, thoughts spiraled around in my brain, knocking into each other. Ma's revelations had completely broadsided me. Ditzy Aunt Sharon, our biological mother? Mind-boggling. For all Ma's faults, I was glad I'd been brought up by her and not her sister. And how hard was it to envisage my father as an adulterer? A cheating husband intent on leaving Ma and taking off with her sister. And then it hit me. He was also going to leave Liz and me. Dad, the parent we always had fun with as children. The parent we went to for advice. The parent who always stuck up for Liz and me when we were in trouble. In our eyes our father was a saint.

How wrong we were.

Ma said she left me with Grandma McKinley for a month when Aunty Sharon died. Which is probably why I remember little of when Ma brought Liz home from the hospital. I was seven at the time, and all my thoughts were on the ancient pony living in the paddock next door to Grandma. The pony's name was Sunbeam and I remember spending all day brushing, riding, feeding, talking to and patting this paragon of fur. So, when I had to leave Grandma's house and go home, a red faced baby sister who pooped and peed in her pants and hurt my ears when she screamed, was poor substitute for a pony.

Walking down the driveway toward the GAP kennels, thermometer in my hand, I looked across at the bedraggled row of tents. No-one around this afternoon. Not a soul. All the residents of Tent City were at a rally to save the earthworms along the Port river banks. Evidently the council had decided to cement a section of the foreshore, thereby trapping earthworms under the mud and leaving them to die a terrible torturous death—according to Spirit, who'd dropped into the house earlier in the day to present me with a small charm sachet she'd made especially for me. She said it contained crushed rose petals, six hairs from a white rabbit's paws, oil of rosemary and other weird stuff I blanked out on. Supposedly, the home-made charm was to prevent me from having bad dreams after coming in contact with two departed souls (aka dead bodies) in a week. Okay, Spirit was an oddball who probably conversed with goblins at the bottom of the garden, but she meant well.

I could see a dark colored Holden sedan parked on the other side of the road just up from me. No-one inside. Maybe the driver was visiting the property over the road. Or the car could have broken down and the driver gone for help.

As I lifted the latch on the kennel-gate, my mobile, jammed deep into my back pocket, started ringing. "Hi handsome," I said, after checking Caller-ID. Instead of two weeks, it felt like years since I'd waved my drop-dead gorgeous boyfriend off on his trip to Victoria. Worth it though. He'd won the final of the Ballarat Cup with one of his favorite greyhounds, *Sheez Magic*, and now had enough money to renovate his kennel house. Something Ben had wanted to do for a long time.

"I'm back," he sang over the phone, and I swear I could hear him panting. "Don't suppose you're alone in that madhouse you call home?"

I slipped a lead onto Ralph, the effervescent dog I was fostering for GAP, and tied him to the fence so I could take his temperature. "Actually, I *am* alone," I told him, in my rusty sex kitten voice. "For the first time in six weeks, I'm blissfully, happily, wonderfully alone."

"Not for long, baby," he purred. "Now—take off your clothes!"

I laughed. "Hold that thought, Lothario. But first, I have some mind-boggling news for you. Can you just hang on a minute while I take Ralph's temperature and then I'll fill you in?"

Eager to get back to Ben, I placed my mobile onto a nearby dog mattress, dug the thermometer from my shirt pocket and leant over Ralph. "Good boy," I told him, rubbing his ears. "You seem fine, but I'd better check you out."

As I slid the thermometer into Ralph's ear, I thought I heard a movement behind me. "Who's that?" I stood, half turned, felt a crashing pain in the back of my head, and then everything went a very painful, disorienting shade of black.

*****

My mouth was so dry, when I tried to swallow, I couldn't. No spit. Felt like someone had stuffed my mouth full of sand. Or gravel. Nothing could get past the dry lump in my throat. And my head? Oh my God. Red hot daggers pierced the back of my skull, digging in deeper and deeper and stirring my brains until I cried out in pain.

What happened? Where was I?

I couldn't see a thing. Everything was black. Scrunched in a ball, I tried to straighten my legs. Couldn't. Nowhere for them to go. When I pushed outwards, my feet hit a rock hard barrier. I reached out with one hand and hit another hard wall. Ran my hand along the wall and up over my body. It was a mere six inches from my head.

Oh God no…surely I wasn't in a coffin. Again. I'd never survive that twice.

My chest, heavy with dread, strained to drag in a deep breath. Nope. The most I could manage was a series of sharp shallow breaths that set my heart racing. If only I could work out where I was. Hunched on my side, knees pulled up to my chest, head throbbing like the worst toothache, I centered my focus.

Okay, it was black, but there were chinks of light showing through some threadlike cracks. So, no, it couldn't be a coffin. And there was a constant thrumming noise. Like the sound of an engine. And systematic vibrations, consistent with a car traveling along a bitumen highway. The smell of motor oil and a mixture of rubber and dirty rags invaded my nostrils.

And then it came to me with a rush of pants-wetting fear. I was trapped in the boot of a car. I closed my eyes and counted to five while I breathed in, held for two and let my breath out slowly to the count of seven.

Keep calm. Don't panic.

Don't panic? Keep calm? Fiddlesticks! Tell that to the marines facing the firing squad. My breath, now out of control, drummed in my ears, drowning out the rhythmical sound of the car motor. I yelled and screamed. Banged both fists on the metal until I felt something wet—blood—running down my arms. It was no good. No-one could hear me. Tears mixing with snot, I slumped back into the fetal position. Whoever used my head as a cricket ball back at the GAP kennels and shoved my inert body in the boot of their car was in all probability, right now, in the process of driving far out into the country to dig a deep hole. And the best I could hope for was that the monster behind the wheel made sure I was dead before he tossed me into the hole and shoveled dirt back over.

It seemed like hours, but was probably only twenty minutes, before

I felt the vibrations of the car change. By the jolting and jouncing, I guessed the driver had turned off the main road onto a bumpy track.

Must be getting close to where X marked the spot.

Strange, but I felt calmer now. More focused. No way was I going to lie there like a limp piece of lettuce and let this murderous goon shoot me and bury me, without a fight. I wiped my nose on my sleeve, steadied my breathing and started an exploration of the boot with my outstretched fingers. Maybe I could find something to use as a weapon. Car boots usually housed helpful things like car-jacks, bowling balls, tools, golf clubs and even the stray rifle.

But not this one…

And then I found it. My weapon of choice. In fact, the *only* weapon at my disposal. It was lying underneath my body, digging into my back, as though asking to be my knight in shining armor.

A heavy metal tire iron.

The car slowed down and the bumps became deeper, indicating we were travelling over rougher terrain. Odds on, it was a remote isolated area eminently suitable for disposing of a too-young-to-die greyhound trainer who just couldn't keep her nose out of murder investigations. I clenched my teeth and gripped the tire iron more firmly.

And then the car hit another bump, deeper than the others, smashing my already aching head against unforgiving metal. The car slowed to a stop. I blinked away stars, ordered my tear ducts to hold the moisture for later, and tightened my grip on the iron.

Plan A—in fact, my only plan—catch this guy by surprise. When he opened the boot, I'd come out swinging, aim for the testicles, which should be at the perfect height to connect.

That was it. Just aim for *the boys*—and then get out of the boot and run like hell.

I shook the stars from my head and the pain out of my focus and lay, scrunched in a stiff ball, waiting.

And waiting…

What the heck was the bad guy doing out there? Having a glass of wine and a picnic with friends before killing me? I eased the tire iron down beside me, wiped my sweaty hands on my jeans, and then took another, firmer grip.

That's when I heard it.

The sound of a key turning in the boot.

Show time!

I tensed, ready for action. I'd only get the one chance. My worst nightmare was out there, primed to lodge a bullet in my brain or a knife in my heart. If I didn't swing with all my strength the moment the boot opened wide enough, I'd be dead meat. Slimy maggot food.

Heart jostling with my tonsils, I watched the lid of the car-boot begin to lift slowly upwards. My eyes squinted against the sudden light after the darkness, my grip tightened around the tire iron…

And then I made my move. "Okay, you piece of dog-shit with maggots for sprinkles," I screamed, swinging the tire iron and aiming for the most vulnerable point between the man's legs. "Take that!"

"Heyy!" The startled man leaped to the right, caught the tire iron on the top of his left leg and bent double in obvious pain.

"Woohoo! That's my girl," said the hot-looking guy standing behind him.

I gaped up at the two men.

The first man, grabbing the top of his leg and grunting some very creative obscenities was none other than Detective Inspector Garry Adams.

And the second man?

A beaming, good-enough-to-eat, arms-open-wide, Benjamin Taylor.'

21

"Sorry, babe, but I reckon you should go to hospital."

I shook my head and cuddled into Ben's chest. His familiar earthy smell and warm comforting arms doing more to ease my uncontrollable shaking than any hospital could.

"But you'll need a dozen or so stitches in that," he persisted, inspecting the painful gash on the back of my head.

"Can't the paramedics stitch me up?"

"They said you need to see a doctor."

"But I just want to go home."

Beside us, a frazzled ambulance attendant attempted to ply the DI with ice packs to the fast-growing bruise on the top of his left leg. "Sit down, Mr. Adams," she said, and pushed him back onto a chair. "And please, stop pulling your trousers up. We need to get ice onto that leg."

"It's not *Mr.* Adams…it's *Detective Inspector*." The DI told the bobbing attendant and then glared across at me. "Why didn't you look before you swung that thing?"

"Why didn't you say who you were before opening the boot?"

Ben grinned at the detective. "And I'm just thankful you shoved me out of the way when I offered to look in the boot first."

"Thank you, but I have no time for this now." The DI stood, brushed the paramedic away, pulled up his trousers and did all the necessary things to make his trousers tidy again. "I'll ice my leg when I get back to the station. At the moment, I have a three-time murderer…almost four…to charge and lock up for a long, long time." He turned to me and shook his head. "You are so lucky, Katrina."

Lucky? I sniffed and dug my fingers into Ben's arm. I'd come so close to being buried in a shallow grave in the middle of nowhere. So close to never seeing my beloved dogs again. And so close to missing out on spending the rest of my life with the man I loved.

"You can thank that boyfriend of yours," went on the DI nodding his head. "He realized something was wrong when he saw a car pulling away from your place and found your mobile abandoned in the kennels. After alerting me, Ben followed the car and kept me informed as to where he was heading. And it looks like we arrived in the nick of time."

Still cuddled into Ben, I looked across at the man in the back of a police car, wrists shackled, and an armed constable on each side of him. Blonde, fortyish, dressed in a business suit. "But who *is* he?" I shrugged, bewildered. "I've never seen that man before in my life. Why did he want to kill me?"

"Same reason he killed the other three, I guess. You were asking too many questions, snooping around, and he couldn't have that happening." The DI shook his head and pulled a notebook from his pocket. "He's Albert Cook, the CEO of the new greyhound-formulation company, *Hounded*."

"Why does the name of that greyhound-food keep coming up? My local vet, Terry Blackburn, asked me if I was feeding my dogs, *Hounded*. I told him I only fed it to the two GAP dogs I'm fostering at the moment, mainly because I'd won a bag of the stuff at the Gawler track."

"Terry Blackburn has been a tremendous help to us in solving this case. He researched the suspect product, *Hounded*. Said caffeine had been added to make the dogs run faster, but as that's a banned substance, a dangerous chemical was also added, to mask the caffeine. Evidently quite a few dogs were allergic to the added chemical and became sick, some dying. Dr. Blackburn rang this morning to inform me of his conclusive findings." The DI crossed his arms and leant back against the side of the ambulance. "Since then, we've been on the look-out for our friend, Mr. Albert Cook, who is currently occupying a police car, to question him on suspicion of murder and using a prohibited and dangerous substance on canine athletes. Couldn't find him anywhere. No-one at the factory or warehouses knew where he'd gone. So while all the *Hounded* laboratories around the country went into chaos, the CEO, who is also their principal chemist, went into hiding."

"But he couldn't resist taking care of me before he disappeared, forever."

The DI's eyes twinkled and he actually smiled. "Yeah…his biggest mistake."

Ben laughed and his arm around my shoulder tightened. "If we'd known your dastardly plan, Kat, we would have insisted the thug open the boot first, before arresting him. Ooh, I'd have loved to see the color of the guy's face when that tire iron connected with his family jewels."

I took another peek at the man locked up in the back of the police car. How close had I come to being this guy's next victim? I sent him a murderous glare. Creep. He turned his head and raised one eyebrow at me. "Hey," I said to the DI. "I *have* seen that man before. He was working on my new kennel-house the day Tinkerbelle was murdered." I looked again and frowned. "In fact, he was the Supervisor. No wonder he sent the other workmen off-site due to some fabricated asbestos scare. He must have stayed behind, in hiding, waiting for a chance to smash a shovel over poor Tinkerbelle's head."

"You're spot on," said the DI.

"But I still don't understand *why* he killed Tinkerbelle, Babette and Steve?" I shook my head. "What was his motive?"

"Our boy sang like a canary when we nailed him. Probably thinks he'll get a more lenient sentence if he talks—which I won't be advocating." Adams shoved both hands into his long trench coat pocket and took a breath. "In the well-connected world of demonstrators and antis, there's not much that gets past those women. Tinkerbelle discovered what was going on with this new super-greyhound-food. In fact, she had proof—a lab report she'd stolen—so of course she had to be eliminated. Unfortunately for Babette, she heard Tinkerbelle talking on the phone to Mr. Cook, blackmailing him for a large sum of money. When Tinkerbelle met her fate, Babette stupidly hunted through Tinkerbelle's belongings, found the lab report, and threatened to go to the police if Cook didn't come up with a million dollars."

"And then Steve was blinded by dollar signs too?"

"Exactly." The DI punched Ben lightly on the arm. "Now, while I make sure this two-bit creep waiting in the police-car is tossed into a jail cell, you, my friend, need to drive your girlfriend to a hospital. Pronto." He raised one eyebrow and his eyes twinkled. "In fact, if you intend sticking with this one, you'll definitely need to win a lot of races in the future to pay for the highest Private Medical cover available."

I acted like any mature rational grown-up and poked my tongue out at him.

22

MY FRONT LAWN LOOKED DESOLATE. Forlorn. Tent City and its occupants had packed up and moved on overnight. All that was left of the vibrancy they'd created over the last six weeks was a black circle from their open fire and flattened grass where tents had once stood.

No baby Charlotte playing under the sprinklers. No late night chanting, 'Save the whale! Save the whale!' to keep me awake. No Mystique and Spirit with their magic herbs and disruptive de-cluttering.

I never thought I'd say this—but I actually missed them.

Liz and Scott came barreling through the front doorway, each with a large backpack strapped to their shoulders and Ben, who'd dropped in earlier, mooching along behind them.

One arm hooked through Scott's, my sister grinned across at me. "Hey, sis, don't tell me you're pining my ditzy friends?"

I returned her grin. "Yep, but don't worry, it's only a fleeting emotion. I predict it will have completely disappeared by the time I finish breakfast."

She laughed. It sounded like the gush of a waterfall. Happy. Confident. I think my baby sister was finally growing up. She'd made peace with Ma and found a man she could get along with. Not that I approved of the bearded scruff who'd finally found the rest of his clothes and decided it was time to come to life again. I only hoped he'd stick with Liz during the back-breaking job of fruit picking and not go running home to his Mummy and Daddy the moment things got hard.

There again, Liz might get up one morning and decide she was bored with the life she was leading, leave Scott with his head in a fruit bin and take off on her own to Antarctica. Just to make sure hunters weren't taking pot-shots at the polar bears.

And if she did…it was her life.

"Well," I said throwing my arms around my sister and hugging her tight. "Keep in touch, this time. I want to hear from you at least once a week."

"How about once a month? And Scott and I'll be back for Christmas dinner?"

I sighed, rubbed at the bandage on my head. Guess that was as good as I was going to get from her. "Okay." I pulled back and narrowed my eyes. "But if I haven't heard from you by the end of the month, I'll come to Queensland with a big stick hunting for you. Okay?"

She smiled and I could see tears threatening.

I turned to Scott. "And you be careful. No more mixing with bad guys who try to put you to sleep in your car, forever. I won't always be around to save your scrawny bones. Okay?"

He leant forward and wrapped me in a bear hug, so tight, I could barely breathe. "Thanks for everything, Kat. After almost dying a couple of months ago, I needed this time to build up my strength again."

"Um…thass okay," I mumbled into his chest.

"You know, it's not every day your life flashes before your eyes and you come close to dying. But thanks to you, I now have a second chance." His hug increased, until I had to beat him on the back, demanding he let me up for air.

"Phew!" I snatched a breath and shook my head at him. "I'd say, you've definitely regained your strength, Scott. Sure you're not related to a boa- constrictor?"

As Ben and I stood at the front door and watched Liz and Scott toss their backpacks into the back of the van and then climb inside, I sniffed and wiped my eyes. I'd liked having my baby sister back in my life. There was plenty of room in my house for her to stay, but I knew it was like caging a wild animal. Liz and I were chalk and cheese. She needed to be free. Free to travel wherever life took her. I needed security and to live in one place, doing a job I loved.

I felt Ben's arm close around me, warming my insides and making me feel better. I snuggled deep into his sweater, smelling dog, rain and the woodsy deodorant he wore that suited his outdoor lifestyle.

Waving, we followed the rusty Kombi van as it rattled down the driveway and out through the front gate. Ben closed the gate behind them and fastened the lock while I crossed to the GAP kennels to have a chat with Ralph and Yolo. Our brilliant local vet, Terry Blackburn, had not only discovered the toxic chemical in *Hounded*, but he'd also brought Yolo's temperature down and saved her life. So, although not quite as bouncy as Ralph at the moment, she was going to be okay.

Ben took my hand as we headed up the driveway. "Do you realize, for the first time in six weeks, we have the house to ourselves."

"That we do."

"And I have a few new moves I'm itching to show you."

"New moves?"

Ben stopped in the middle of the driveway and turned me to him. His kiss was so sweet it took my breath away. And then it deepened and I wanted to climb inside of him.

He sucked in a shaky breath as he slowly pulled away. "Oh God, let's go upstairs to your bedroom before I take you right here in the middle of the driveway, in full view of every passing motorist."

My breath was just as shaky. "Don't know if I can last that long, the driveway looks pretty comfortable to me."

"No, no, no. Believe me when I say, what I'm aiming to do with you Katrina McKinley, would be much better accomplished in the comfort of a bed."

He grabbed my hand and, laughing, we started to run. I even had my fingers around the front door handle when the roar of a motorbike brought us to a stop.

I peeked over my shoulder. Was that a Harley idling in front of my gateway? A leather-clad biker drawing back the latch and waving to us?

Unable to contain my Cheshire-cat grin, I watched as a black and chrome Harley, shinier than a teacher's apple, growled its way down the driveway, bit dirt, and then reared to a flashy halt beside us.

The rider, clad in black leather with a Red Dragon emblem in pride of place on his sleeveless jacket and arms buried in tattoos, peered at us through his faceless black helmet. He rolled his massive shoulders and switched off the engine. His pillion passenger, also covered in black leather, removed her helmet, revealing an equally large woman in her mid-thirties.

Ben growled deep in his throat beside me. His arm snaked around my shoulders in a death-grip of ownership. "Can I please shoot him?"

The biker dismounted. An alien creature, with shoulders like an ox and legs like two-hundred-year old tree stumps. Then, slowly, with great aplomb, he straightened to his full height of almost seven-foot, removed his helmet and placed it on the seat of his ultra-powerful hog. Throwing out his massive chest, he cranked his shoulders and shook his head at me. "Still with this bozo, Katrina?"

For a moment, Ben glared at the big man's red and black bandana, nose-ring, matching eye-brow rings and shaved head, then, teeth gritted together in what could only be called a snarl, he dragged me even closer. "Yes, she is, Biker Boy. Now, go away!"

I refused to be part of this Mexican stand-off. Wriggling out of Ben's vice-like grip, I sent him a quick I-can't-believe-you're being-so-rude eye-roll then turned and grinned up at the craggy face with that idiotic sparse ginger beard. "Scuzz?"

"Katrina." And with a bellow that would do a bull proud, Scuzz—or as it declared on his birth certificate, Theodore Samuel Parkington the Third—took two giant steps forward and scooped me up off the ground in a monster hug, twirled me around twice and put me gently back on the ground.

My eyes were level with the shiny metal tag in the middle of his jacket zipper. I could see the rise and fall of his chest. Smell his expensive cologne mixed with the strangely comforting scent of engine oil. And feel the roughness of his fingers as he cupped my chin and forced my head back to meet his eyes.

"Katrina, darling girl. It's been far too long. Let me look at you," he said and I swear it felt like he was eating my body with his gaze. "Every day since I left, I've thought about you."

"No, you haven't," growled Ben and it wouldn't have surprised me if he'd stamped his foot. "She's mine!"

I glared at Ben. What was the matter with him? Scuzz was our good friend. "Oh Scuzz, it's good to see you too, but remember—I'm spoken for."

"Humph! Only if you say so."

I dragged my eyes away from the gorgeous hunk of a man who'd always been like a giant box of chocolates to me. Tempting, but off limits. Only a few months ago, I'd almost succumbed to Scuzz's inner beauty and outer ruggedness, back when he was my bodyguard. Not only had he protected me when I was vulnerable, but he'd also risked his life to rescue my greyhounds when a cold-hearted murderer set fire to my kennel house. And for that, I could never thank him enough.

During all this, the woman astride the pillion seat of the Harley had been quietly following our antics. She looked to be holding back a grin with an effort. "Theodore," she said at last, her voice slightly disgruntled. "Aren't you going to introduce me to your friends?"

Scuzz turned to the woman in black leather. "Sorry," he said in his private school voice—the one that sounded like he was born with a silver spoon in his over-large mouth. "Katrina, Ben, this is my half-sister, Thunder. She's a cop, an expert with a gun and so strong she can lift villains off the ground with one hand and toss them over a cliff."

I smiled at her. "Sounds impressive."

She returned the smile. "My half-brother tends to exaggerate."

"So I've noticed."

Scuzz picked up both my hands and studied my fingers. "Hey, cowboy, where's the ring?" He lifted one eyebrow at Ben. "You know, until there's a ring on Katrina's finger, she's still up for grabs."

"Up for grabs?" I repeated, shaking my head at them. This had gone far enough. "Excuse me, you two, but I'm not a possession, something to be fought over and the winner gets to keep me shackled to the kitchen sink."

Ben took a step closer and glared writhing snakes up at the leather clad biker. "Listen, Scuzz, she's *my* girl and I don't want you pawing her, okay?"

"There's no ring yet, cowboy."

I sighed. May as well not have spoken, just gone inside and had a cup of coffee and left them to it.

Ben sent Scuzz another writhing-snakes scowl. "Okay, you've forced me into this. I *was* going to perform in the privacy of our bedroom, but since you've got your greasy hands all over my girl, I'll do it right now. Right here. And you and Thunder can be my witnesses." He turned to me and his voice softened. "Katrina?"

What in the name of Zeus and all his dead babies was going on here? Surely Ben wasn't going to show me his 'moves'. Not out here on my front porch, where Scuzz and Thunder and any passing motorist could cop an eyeful?

I inched away from him. Felt my face blaze in embarrassment. Experimenting with Kama Sutra moves in the privacy of our bedroom was what I lived for—out here in public—not so much.

Nervously, I watched Ben reach into his back pocket and produce what looked like a small box. He took a deep breath as though to settle himself down before gazing at me with a determined glint in his eye. "Babe," he said, and cleared his throat, "I *was* going to ask you after a marathon bout of two-weeks-away-from-you, sex. You know, while we were all loved up. But now, just to show this big tattooed biker nerd he's been completely wiped from the program, I'll propose to you right here and now."

I blinked, felt my jaw drop. Did I hear Ben just say the word, propose? *Propose*—as in…

"Okay, this is a tad awkward and not quite how I imagined proposing, but Kat, I love your smile, your loyalty, your big heart. I love everything about you." Ignoring the sharp gravel, Ben gave his jeans a slight hitch before dropping down on one knee in front of me. "I'm not much at flowery words, but I love you more than life itself and I want to spend the rest of my days proving it to you."

I felt a huge heart-warming smile coming on. *My* Ben was proposing. And wow! For a guy who professed to not being much at flowery words—he was doing it beautifully.

He reached out, clasped my hand as though it was more precious than gold. "Kat, I promise to love you in sickness and in health. For richer or poorer—"

"Hey, cowboy, it's not time to spout your wedding vows yet!" Scuzz threw his arms up in frustration, tut-tutting loudly. "Get on with it," he growled. "Just ask the girl to marry you."

Ignoring the hovering biker's goading, Ben's fingers tightened around mine. "Being with you, means more to me than winning the richest Group 1 race in the world…"

"Oh, Ben, that's so beautiful…"

I could hear Scuzz making exaggerated vomit noises nearby, but all I could see was Ben's eyes, shining with love and tenderness. I sniffed back tears and waited for the strategic words.

"Kat, babe, will you marry me?"

Dear Readers

A former school teacher, competitive horse rider, and greyhound trainer, June Whyte has always dreamed of being an author.

She wrote her first full-length story (with chapters) when she was nine-years-old — *Donald McDonald in Texas* — a story involving a rather extraordinary boy who rode buck-jumpers in a rodeo.

And when she penned her first murder mystery, *Murder Behind Bars*, it resulted in her fifth-grade teacher questioning her home life.

Even now, in retirement, June's favorite spot is sitting in front of her computer, drawing on her knowledge of greyhounds and horses to create humorous mysteries for both adults and younger teens.

Her *Kat McKinley* greyhound series, starting with *Chasing Can Be Murder*, is laugh out loud funny, as is her *Chiana Ryan*, PI, Young Adult mystery series.

She's also written the cozy mystery series, *Vets2U*, which is similar to the TV show, Rosemary & Thyme — but instead of gardeners, Emily and Maggie are veterinarians. This series is for animal lovers — especially those who love horses.

For more information and news, go to:

www.junewhytebooks.com

Thank you,
June Whyte

www.ingramcontent.com/pod-product-compliance
Lightning Source LLC
Chambersburg PA
CBHW031051310726
48969CB00007B/2226